The Happy Hollisters and the Whistle-Pig Mystery

BY JERRY WEST

Illustrated by Helen S. Hamilton

GARDEN CITY, N.Y.

DOUBLEDAY & COMPANY, INC.

Contents

CHAPTER 1

COPS AND ROBBERS

"BLACKIE lost his best friend," said Holly Hollister. "That's why the poor dog won't eat or anything."

The pig-tailed girl, who was six, balanced on the rail fence, which bordered the Hollisters' front yard. On the grass sat her two sisters, dark-haired Sue, four, and blond Pam, ten. The older girl was cross-legged, and in her lap nestled White Nose with her five kittens.

Pam stroked the mother cat. "What about Blackie's friend, the woodchuck?" she asked. "Where did the little creature go?"

The three Hollister girls were fond of Blackie, a cocker spaniel owned by Indy Roades, who worked for Mr. Hollister. Indy's backyard extended into a woods. At the edge of it had lived a perky little woodchuck, whom Blackie used to romp with every day. But the chuck had vanished, and the cocker was moping because he missed his playmate.

"I know what!" Holly exclaimed, leaping down from the fence. "Let's take White Nose and the kittens over to Indy's. Blackie can play with them."

Pam liked the idea. "Maybe Pete and Ricky would want to come," she said. Instantly, Holly raced across the lawn toward their house on the edge of Pine Lake, calling her two brothers. She found seven-year-old Ricky sitting on the front steps with a glass of water beside him. He had a squirt gun in his hand and was having target practice with a scurrying black ant.

"Yikes! Sure, I'd like to come," the red-headed boy declared. He filled his water pistol and tucked it into his belt.

Then Holly ran inside and called Pete, who was twelve and had blond crewcut hair. He was seated before the television in the living room. "Crickets!" he exclaimed. "You should have seen what happened in New England—a train robbery!"

When the older boy joined his brother and sisters in the yard, he told the latest news. A train had been held up near the town of Foxboro, and masked bandits had robbed the mail car of nearly a million dollars in cash. "It was in three U.S. postal sacks," Pete said, and added, "Police have surrounded the whole area."

"I wish we could be there to help 'em," Ricky declared, patting his water pistol. Then he said, "Let's play cops and robbers!"

"Not now," Pam said. "We're going to take White Nose and her kittens to keep Blackie company."

After the Hollisters had walked several long

6

blocks they came to the house where Indy Roades lived. Marching into the backyard, they found Blackie lying on the grass beside his doghouse. The cocker spaniel's head lay on his outstretched front paws and he looked up sadly at the children.

"See, we brought you our cat and kittens to play with," Sue chirped. "Now you won't be lonesome any more, Blackie."

The dog wagged his tail only once. Then he looked sad again. The girls put White Nose and her kittens on the ground and the animals paraded around Blackie. Still he did not show any interest.

"He doesn't want to bother with those silly cats," Ricky declared. "Come on! Let's play cops and robbers! Make believe the train bandits are in the woods here and we're chasing them."

"And we can use Blackie for a bloodhound," suggested Holly, her eyes brightening with the idea.

"You go ahead," Pam said. "I'll stay here and take care of White Nose and her family."

"Me too," piped little Sue.

Pete, Ricky, and Holly ran off into the woods, calling for Blackie to follow. Indy's dog obeyed, but did not seem very peppy.

"Come on, Blackie," Ricky urged. "There are bandits in here!"

Pushing the "bloodhound" along before them, the three children tiptoed along the path. It led deeper into the woods, where the trees were taller and closer together. Ahead there loomed a huge rock. As they passed it, Holly was suddenly pelted by pine cones.

"The robbers!" she cried out, stopping and glancing about her wildly.

"What imagination!" exclaimed Ricky. "Nobody's around here!" Just then a pine cone bounced off his freckled nose. "Yikes, where did that come from?"

Without saying a word, Pete motioned to the huge boulder. It was so high they could not see if anyone were hiding on top of it.

Ricky winked and nodded. He walked softly to a nearby birch sapling and shinnied up it. Soon he was level with the top of the big rock. Pressed flat against it were two husky boys. Their faces were turned away from Ricky, but he recognized them. They were Joey Brill and his friend Will Wilson.

Quietly, the red-haired boy drew his water pistol and aimed it toward the rock. Then he hissed loudly, *"Pstt!"* Joey and Will turned their heads in surprise and as they did, *squirt!* The drops of water hit their faces!

"I got 'em, Pete!" Ricky cried out as he slid down the tree to join the others.

Joey Brill, who always made trouble for the Hollisters, stood up on the rock and shouted at them, "We'll get you for this!"

"Come on down," Pete invited him.

"It's too far to jump," Joey retorted.

"We'll get you for this!"

"Yeah, we have to climb down slowly," Will chimed in.

"That's too bad. We'll see you later," called Pete, and the three children raced back to Indy's house with Blackie loping along ahead of them.

"We got the robbers, all right," Ricky announced with a grin when they joined Pam and Sue. He told them about Joey and Will.

"Now they'll try to get even," Pam said as the girls gathered up the kittens.

"Well, I think we've made Blackie a little happier," Holly remarked, and the children started home again. Soon they entered the driveway of the Hollister property, which lay between the road and the shore of Pine Lake. In the garden beside the large rambling house, they saw their mother picking flowers.

"Some mail came for you, children," she called gaily. "You'll find it on the hall table."

Pam hastened inside and returned with a letter postmarked Germany. Opening it quickly, she found that it was from an old woodcarver they had met on a trip in the Black Forest, where the youngsters had solved a mystery.

"What does it say?" asked Sue, tugging at Pam's skirt.

"Mr. Fritz wants us to do him a favor," Pam said. She explained that the woodcarver needed the dimensions of a certain wooden Indian called The Settlers' Friend. "This is a special statue," Pam con-

10

tinued, "and Mr. Fritz has an order to carve one just like it."

"Crickets!" exclaimed Pete. "Where can we find The Settlers' Friend? It could be in Alaska for all we know!"

"I'll tell you where you might find out," Mrs. Hollister put in, taking off her garden gloves. "Indy Roades makes a hobby of studying wooden Indians. He has a book full of pictures of them."

"Thank you, Mother," Pete said. "Maybe we can see Indy when he goes home for lunch."

The boy hastened into the house and telephoned The Trading Post. This was a combination hardware, sporting goods and toy shop which Mr. Hollister ran in the center of Shoreham. Indy said he would meet them at his home at noon to show them the book on wooden Indians.

When Pete returned to the yard, he saw Ricky leading their pet burro, Domingo, from his stall in the garage while the girls watched. The redhead swung himself onto the burro's back just as a beautiful collie dog ran up, barking excitedly.

"Quiet, Zip!" Holly said, twirling her pigtails. "You can't have a ride. And look at you, all wet! You've been chasing frogs in the lake again!"

The collie shook himself, spraying water all over the girls. Then he raced across the lawn back toward the lake.

Mrs. Hollister prepared an early lunch for Pete and Pam, and when they had finished, the two older children hastened back to Indy's house. Their friend drove up just as they arrived.

Indy Roades was a short, stocky man with jet-black hair and a reddish-tan complexion. He was a real Indian, a member of a Pueblo tribe from New Mexico.

He gave them a big smile as he got out of his car. "So you're interested in wooden Indians, too!" he said. "Come in. I'll show you my book."

Blackie followed them sadly into the house where Indy pulled a large bright-colored volume from a shelf in his living room. Pete and Pam sat on the floor and opened the book.

"Oh, what beautiful colored pictures!" Pam said as they turned page after page showing wooden Indians collected from all over the United States.

"We're looking for one called The Settlers' Friend," Pete explained.

"Oh, here it is!" his sister exclaimed.

The Settlers' Friend wore a feathered war bonnet on his proud head. His chin was firm and jutting and his nose straight as an arrow. In his left hand The Settlers' Friend held a pipe of peace, and in his right one he extended three ears of corn.

Pam read the caption. It said that The Settlers' Friend was in a museum called the Pioneer Village in Foxboro, a town in New England.

"Crickets!" Pete said. "Foxboro! That's where the train robbery happened today!"

"Maybe we can go there," Pam said, "and measure the Indian for Mr. Fritz."

"And find the train robbers as well," Pete declared.

Indy said that they could borrow the book any time they wanted. After he had replaced it on the shelf, he drove the two children back to their house.

Indy went in with them. He wanted to see his friend, Sue. The younger children were in the kitchen having lunch with their mother.

"Oh, Indy! Indy!" Sue cried as she jumped from her chair and ran to meet him.

The man whirled her around a couple of times and placed her on top of his head. "I'm a totem pole!" Sue declared, giggling. Then Indy swung her in a great arc and set her on the floor.

"Mother," Pam said, "we've found where The Settlers' Friend is located—in Foxboro—where the train was robbed."

"Let's all go there!" Ricky exclaimed.

Mrs. Hollister shook her head slowly. "I'm afraid not, children. Neither Daddy nor I can take time off now." The youngsters looked disappointed.

"Oh, gee whizzickers yikes!" Ricky said. "I thought we could solve another mystery and have an adventure."

Indy began to whistle a tune and gaze at the ceiling. "I have a vacation in a few days," he said airily.

13

Holly flung her arms around the Indian. "Then you can take us!" she squealed.

Mrs. Hollister smiled and said, "But how will you manage all five children, Indy?"

"Well, there's Snow Flower," their friend said with a smile.

"Snow Flower? What's that?" asked Holly.

"My sister," Indy replied. "Her friends call her Emmy, but her Indian name is Snow Flower. She's coming here to visit me. Maybe she and I could take you youngsters to Foxboro."

"Oh, Mother, please say yes!" begged Pam.

Mrs. Hollister laughed. "If Snow Flower is willing, it's all right with me."

Sue hugged her mother while Ricky and Holly jumped around making Indian war whoops at the prospect of going on a trip. The children's happiness continued all day.

That evening Pete got his basketball, and he and Ricky went to shoot baskets in front of the garage. Domingo, in his stall, looked out at the two boys. Every time Ricky missed, the burro went "Eee-yaw!"

"He makes me nervous," Ricky complained. "That's why I can't shoot so well."

"That's okay," Pete said as he lifted a one-hand shot through the ring. "You did pretty well with your squirt gun this morning."

When it grew too dark to see the basket, Pete placed the ball alongside the garage, then he and his brother went into the house. Shortly afterward Pete got a telephone call from Dave Mead, his best friend. He was Pete's age and lived nearby.

"Say, I hear you're going to Foxboro!" said Dave.

"How did you find out?"

"Holly spread the news around," Dave replied with a chuckle. He added, "My parents know a family in Foxboro."

"Really?" Pete asked. "Who are they?"

"You and Pam come on over and we'll talk about it," Dave said.

The older children told their father where they were going and why. Mr. Hollister, who was a tall, athletic-looking man, said, "All right, don't be too late." Then he grinned and added, "I see you're starting on your detective work already—those train robbers had better watch out."

Laughing, Pete and Pam left the house. As they hurried past their garage, they heard a noise.

"Zip? Is that you?" Pam asked. No reply. Then Domingo brayed.

Pete stopped and whispered, "Do you suppose someone's prowling around here, Pam?"

He had hardly spoken when—*thump!* Something hit Pete hard on the head.

CHAPTER 2

A SPOOKY SEARCH

PETE let out a startled cry as his own basketball bounced off his head. He whirled about and looked up. In the darkness he could make out the form of Joey Brill kneeling on top of the garage.

"There! I got even!" the bully called. He ran to the edge of the roof and quickly let himself down over the side while Pete went to retrieve the basketball. By the time he returned with it, Joey had slipped away into the darkness.

"Are you hurt?" Pam asked.

"No, I'm okay," her brother replied, and put the ball in the garage. "Come on, let's see what Dave Mead's parents have to say about Foxboro."

It was only a five-minute walk to Dave's house, but to save time Pete and Pam cut through a vacant lot behind the Mead property and knocked at Dave's back door.

"Hi," said Dave. "I thought you'd come this way." The tall, straight-haired boy led them through the kitchen and into the living room where his mother and father sat reading.

"Oh, hello, Pete, Pam," Mrs. Mead said. Her

husband, a short, squarely built man, looked up from his paper and nodded at the callers.

"We hear you're going to Foxboro," he said.

"You'll like it there," his wife went on. "Especially at the Pioneer Village." She explained that the place was made up of historic old buildings which had been moved to the museum grounds.

"And you know people in Foxboro?" Pam asked.

"Yes, the Culvers," Mrs. Mead replied. "They're old friends of ours. They have a little girl about Holly's age."

"Oh, that's nice," Pam said. "What is she like?"

"She's a darling, but . . ." Mrs. Mead hesitated.

"But what?" Pam asked.

"Well—you may find out for yourself, but I hope not. After all," Dave's mother continued, "she could have changed by now."

Pete and Pam were perplexed. "Why all the mystery?" Pete wondered to himself. Pam was just about to ask a few questions when Mrs. Mead excused herself to make a telephone call.

"Let's watch the news," Dave's father suggested, and reached over to switch on the television. The first item the announcer read was about the mail train robbery at Foxboro. Pictures were shown of the town and Pioneer Village, too. A big white frame house appeared on the screen.

"This is the famous Stagecoach Inn," the newscaster said. The scene switched to the interior of the old structure. The viewers saw a large hall with

17

a row of wooden Indians on either side. But the picture changed before Pete and Pam could identify The Settlers' Friend. The announcer went on to say, however, that the carved figures were rare and valuable.

When the broadcast was over, Mr. Mead shut off the set. "Hmmm," he said, "I didn't know that wooden Indians are valuable."

"Indy Roades has a book about them," Pam told him. "Some of those old ones are worth quite a bit of money."

"I know where there's a wooden Indian," Mr. Mead said.

"You do? Where, Dad?" Dave spoke up.

"I meant to tell you about it when I came home from the office tonight," the boy's father said.

Mr. Mead, who worked for the public utility company in Shoreham, told the children that one of his men had gone into the cellar of an empty house to remove a gas meter.

"The people who used to live there are about to sell the place," he said, "so we removed their meter, which needed repairing." He explained that the workman had reported seeing a wooden Indian in the basement.

"Do you suppose we could get a look at it?" Dave asked his father.

"Of course. Why don't you all come down to my office tomorrow, and I'll find out where it is."

"That'd be keen," Pete said.

"I think we'd better go now," Pam put in. She noticed that Mrs. Mead was still on the telephone and added, "Please say good night for us."

"Right," Dave said. "I'll pick you up at nine tomorrow morning."

Pete and Pam left the Meads' home and started across the vacant lot. Suddenly there was a rustling noise in the bushes ahead.

"If that's Joey Brill, he's not going to fool me again!" Pete whispered. A moment later the figure of a boy burst out of the brush. With a flying tackle Pete brought him down, and they rolled over and over on the ground.

"Hey, let me up! What's the big idea?" cried Ricky. Surprised, Pete let go.

"So it's only you!" he said with a chuckle and helped his brother to his feet.

"What are you doing here, Ricky?" Pam asked him.

"Foxboro and the Pioneer Village and the Stagecoach Inn! They were on television!" Ricky said, out of breath. "The Meads' phone was busy so I ran over to tell you myself!"

"We know," said Pam. "We saw them. But thanks, anyway."

As they walked home, Pete told of the wooden Indian which one of Mr. Mead's workmen had seen in an old cellar.

"Yikes! That sounds spooky!" Ricky exclaimed. "Do you suppose it's valuable like the others?"

"What's the big idea?" cried Ricky.

"Crickets!" Pete said. "I hope so."

"I think wooden Indians are keen," Ricky declared as they trotted past their garage and headed for the house.

The next morning Pete and Pam had not yet finished eating breakfast when Dave arrived.

"Are you ready to go Indian-hunting?" he asked with a big grin, as he walked into the Hollister dining room.

Pete drank the rest of his milk, folded his napkin and rose from the table. "I'm with you, Dave."

"Me too," said Pam. "Do you suppose we'll need a flashlight?"

"Yes," Dave said. "Might be pretty dark down there, especially if it's an old house."

As Pam went to get a flashlight, Holly and Ricky clamored to join in the adventure, but Mrs. Hollister spoke up. "I have several chores for you two," she said, smiling. "I'm afraid I can't spare you this morning."

Holly and Ricky looked disappointed, but Pete said, "If we find anything unusual, maybe we can phone you to come over later."

"Don't forget," Holly said with a small pout.

"If you get in trouble, just let us know," said Ricky, throwing out his chest.

"Nothing will scare us," Pete assured him.

A few minutes later he, Pam and Dave started walking to town. When they reached the public utilities building Dave led them to the elevator and they got off at the fourth floor.

"There's Dad's office, over this way," the dark-haired boy said.

Mr. Mead, who was seated behind a desk, rose to greet them. "You came just in time," he said. "I have been talking to Mike, one of our repairmen. He has a job several doors away from the Quinns' old home, and he'll take you over if you care to ride in the company truck."

Pete looked at his sister. She grinned and nodded vigorously. "Okay, let's go then," Dave's father said. He took them down in the elevator and out to the back of the building where a jolly-looking man in overalls was introduced to them as Mike.

"Drop them off at the Quinns' place, Mike. The cellar door is open, so they can take a look around. I'm sure the Quinns won't mind." Mr. Mead explained that the owners, an elderly couple, had gone to live in an apartment house.

"Fine," Mike said with a twinkle. "I think we can all squeeze in front if Pam sits on one of your laps. Whose will it be?"

"Dave's, of course," Pete replied with a grin, and his sister blushed. When they were all in the truck, Dave set his jaw and did not say a word during the entire trip.

Mike drove them to a small street in the older part of town. He stopped in front of a tiny gray house. As Pam got out, she saw that the curtains and shades had been taken down and the property had a deserted look.

"Can you get home by yourselves?" Mike asked.

"Crickets, of course!" Pete replied, and added, "Thanks for the ride, Mike."

"Glad to help," the workman said cheerfully and drove on.

A strong breeze ruffled Pam's hair as she, Pete, and Dave hurried around to the back of the house. There they saw an old-fashioned cellar door, the kind that children can slide on. Pete and Dave opened the two halves of the door as far as the rusty hinges would allow.

Pete led the way down a short flight of stone steps to an inner door. He opened it and the damp, musty smell of an earthen cellar floor drifted out to greet them.

"This place must be a hundred years old!" Dave said. Pam flashed on her light and swept it around the gloomy interior.

They walked forward cautiously, and Pam brushed the cobwebs from her hair. Then the flashlight beam settled on a narrow open doorway in one wall. Pam shone the light inside and saw a small room with several empty chip baskets in it.

"That must have been a fruit cellar," Pete said. "People had them in old-fashioned houses." The three children went on past a big black furnace. Suddenly there was a terrific *bang* and the cellar grew darker.

"Oh!" Pam exclaimed. "What was that?"

"I guess one of the outside doors blew shut," Dave declared. He added impatiently, "Say, where is this wooden Indian anyway?"

The flashlight probed the musty corners but nowhere could the statue be seen.

"Maybe someone came here before us and took it," Pam said.

"The workman saw it only yesterday," Dave reminded her.

"Listen," Pete said. "If the other side of that heavy cellar door falls, we may be trapped in here. I'm going to make sure that they both stay open."

"I'll help you," offered Dave.

"Okay. I'll keep looking for the Indian," Pam said. The two boys mounted the stone steps and pushed back the door which had fallen.

As they did, Pam's flashlight came to rest on a tall thin panel. "Could this be a closet?" she asked herself. "Oh yes, there's a door knob on it."

Her fingers grasped the cold knob and she pulled the panel open. Then she flashed her light up. The beam came to rest on a fierce face glaring at her. Pam screamed.

CHAPTER 3

THE CROSSPATCH INDIAN

PAM's shriek brought both boys running back to her.

"Oh!" She drew a deep breath, her pulse pounding. "It's—it's only the wooden Indian. He scared me!"

"I can see why," Pete remarked, gazing at the fierce-looking face. In the glare of the flashlight, the high cheekbones cast deep shadows in the eye sockets, and the turned-down mouth looked frightening. Besides, the savage held a tomahawk raised in his left hand. At his right side, with the butt resting on the base of the statue, was a wooden rifle.

"This is no friendly Indian!" Dave remarked. "No wonder they kept him stowed away in a closet."

"Let's get him out," said Pete.

The two boys tugged and twisted, finally working the figure out of its niche, then set it upright on the cellar floor. "I wonder if we could have it," Dave said as he blew some of the dust from the Indian's shoulders. Pam suggested that they get in touch with Mr. and Mrs. Quinn, who owned the statue.

"I'll telephone them," Pete volunteered.

"Okay," Dave said. "We'll stand guard on the Indian."

Pete climbed the cellar steps and took a deep breath of fresh air as he emerged into the sunshine. He trotted off down the street and two blocks farther on came to a corner candy store which had a telephone booth. Pete opened the directory to the Q's and his finger went down the column of names, finally coming to five Quinns.

"Crickets!" Pete said to himself. "I don't have enough change to call all of them." The boy turned to the storekeeper and inquired about the elderly couple who had moved away.

"The name was Peter J. Quinn," the man told him.

Pete grinned. "Same name as mine," he said and quickly found the right number. A woman with a quavering voice answered the telephone.

"This is Pete Hollister," the boy said. "My sister Pam and I and a friend named Dave Mead have just seen the wooden Indian in the cellar of your old house. It may be valuable and we wondered . . ."

Pete was interrupted by the voice on the other end, and as he listened, a delighted expression crossed his face. "You mean it? We can have it?" he asked. "For nothing? Oh, thank you, Mrs. Quinn!" he exclaimed and hung up. Pete raced all the way back to the old house and arrived breathless in the dank cellar. "We can have the Indian!" he shouted.

"You got permission from the Quinns?" asked Pam, still holding the flashlight.

"I'll say I did!" Pete went on happily. "Mrs. Quinn said she didn't ever want to see that old Indian again. It scared the wits out of her. That's why she had it put away in the closet."

"But how will we get it home?" Pam wondered.

Pete snapped his fingers. "I have an idea. If we can get Ricky's coaster wagon and Donna Martin's, too, we could put them together and lay the wooden Indian over the top. We could drag it home that way!"

"Okay," said Pam. "I'll call this time." She raced off to telephone Ricky while the two boys remained in the old house. Before long she came skipping back with the news that Ricky, Holly, Donna Martin and Jeff and Ann Hunter all were coming over to help. They were bringing *three* coaster wagons.

"Oh, boy! That'll be great!" declared Dave.

While they waited, Pam looked about the cellar and found an old cloth, with which she dusted the wooden Indian thoroughly. Still he looked dull and grimy.

"You need a bath," Pam told the scowling savage.

"Look," Dave remarked. "The rifle can be lifted right out of the Indian's hand."

Pete removed the wooden weapon and carried it

outdoors where he and Dave examined it in day-light.

"Crickets! This looks just like the real thing," Pete said as Pam joined them. After admiring the gun, the three sat on the cellar steps to wait for their friends. Nearly half an hour had passed when shouts of laughter came from far down the street. Pam jumped up and ran to the curb. "Here they come with the wagons!" she called as she looked down the road.

The five children came marching along, singing gaily as they pulled the three coasters. In one of them rode Sue.

When they drew closer, Pam saw that the Hollisters' wagon had several long pieces of rope in it.

"We've come to capture an Indian!" Ricky announced stoutly as the procession entered the back-yard.

"Good," Pete said. "Come on. You can give us a hand with this fierce warrior."

"This is fun!" said Donna, who was Holly's friend. Her plump cheeks were pink with excitement.

"Tell us what to do," said curly-haired Ann Hunter who was Pam's best friend. Ann's eight-year-old brother Jeff said nothing, but his blue eyes were sparkling.

"Ann," said Pete, "you and Donna and Jeff tie the wagons end to end. The rest of you come with me."

When the others had followed him into the cellar, Pete replaced the rifle. Then he and Dave eased the wooden Indian down, and eager hands carried the heavy relic up into the daylight.

"The wagons are ready," Ann announced.

"Okay," Dave said. "Lay it down easy."

The wooden Indian covered two and a half wagons! Soon the figure was lashed tightly in place.

"Hey, we ought to give this fellow a name," Dave suggested as the wagon train started to leave the yard.

"He looks like a wild Apache," Pam said.

"I like Patchy," piped Sue.

Hearing this, the others laughed and Pam said, "That's good. Let's call him Patchy. He looks like a crosspatch, anyhow."

As the wagon wheels bounced over cracks in the sidewalk, the rifle jiggled by the Indian's side.

"Pete," said Ricky, "I'd like to carry that gun for awhile. May I?"

"All right," Pete replied, "but don't fool around with it. That rifle's a part of the statue, and we don't want to lose it."

"I'll be careful," his brother promised.

Pete and Dave slid the rifle barrel through Patchy's right hand and handed the firearm to Ricky. With a grin the redhead shouldered it, threw out his chest and marched ahead.

All the other children took turns pulling and

"I like Patchy," piped Sue.

pushing the wagons, which moved slowly along. Passers-by stopped to smile at the sight.

"Where are you going to bury Chief Rain-in-the-Face?" one man called out to them.

"Good gracious!" remarked a woman. "I see you've captured Sitting Bull!"

"He's too tired to sit any more," Holly said impishly. "That's why he's lying down."

As the jolly procession reached Shoreham Road, Joey Brill rode up on his bicycle.

"What have you got there?" he called out.

"A crosspatch Indian!" replied Sue.

Joey pedaled closer as if to look at the figure, but instead he had his eye on the wooden rifle which Ricky carried. Then, so quickly that Pete could not stop him, Joey reached out with one hand and pulled the weapon from Ricky's shoulder.

"Stop that!" Ricky cried, hanging onto the gun stock with both hands. Joey jerked the barrel and pedaled ahead, but Ricky still hung on, half running, half dragged along the sidewalk.

"Let go yourself!" Joey yelled. He turned to glare at Ricky, but in doing so ran straight into a tree. He sprawled headfirst on the grass between the sidewalk and the street, and let go of the rifle. Ricky grabbed it and ran back to the others.

"Look what you did! You made me crack up!" Joey said spitefully as he rose to his feet and picked up the bicycle.

"You did it yourself," Pete retorted. "Don't blame my brother."

Just then Officer Cal, the young policeman who was the Hollisters' friend, drove past in his patrol car. When Joey saw him he quickly hopped on his bicycle and raced off.

"Look, Officer Cal, we have an old Indian!" Holly called.

"And a rifle too!" said Ricky.

The policeman stopped the car, stepped out and looked at the figure tied to the wagons. "Looks like this fellow put up a hard fight," the officer said with a grin.

Pete laughed. "No," he said, "but Ricky did. He rescued the rifle."

"I think Joey might try to take it again," Ann Hunter put in.

"Then I'll give you a police escort right to your house," Officer Cal offered. He got back into the patrol car, and drove slowly alongside them until they hauled the wooden Indian onto the Hollister property. Then as the children called their thanks the policeman waved and drove off.

"Let's keep Patchy here at your house," Dave said.

"That's fine," Pam replied. "I'll wash him good with soap and water."

Mrs. Hollister came out to watch while Ann Hunter helped Pam clean the old wooden Indian. When they had finished, his red, gold and green colors shone brightly.

"Patchy is quite a dandy," Mrs. Hollister remarked as she gazed at the Indian standing in the middle of their lawn.

One hour later, when Mr. Hollister drove home for lunch, he acted frightened by the fierce-looking figure. "Do you think he'll hurt me, Sue?" he asked, stepping out of the car.

"Oh, Daddy! He's only wooden!" the little girl said. "See?" She walked up close to Patchy and patted him.

"I've got an idea," Pete said. "Why don't we put the Indian in front of The Trading Post this afternoon? It might attract a lot of customers."

"Good idea," his father said, and hurried into the house to telephone Indy Roades.

"Hello, Indy," Mr. Hollister said with a chuckle. "I'd like you to bring the truck over. There's a fellow tribesman of yours who wants to see The Trading Post."

Indy was puzzled at what his employer had said, and brought the pickup truck in a hurry. When he saw Patchy, he grinned broadly.

Later in the afternoon the sidewalk in front of Mr. Hollister's Trading Post in downtown Shoreham was crowded with people. They were gazing at the wooden Indian, who stood there looking fiercely at them with tomahawk in one hand and rifle in the other. The Hollister children stood on the side and watched.

One man said, "I'll bet this is the only wooden Indian in town."

When Sue heard the remark she walked into the store and tugged at her father's hand. "Daddy," she said, "don't you think that Patchy will get lonesome?"

"Well, maybe. What do you have in mind?"

"Maybe he'd be happier with all those other wooden Indians."

"He might be," Mr. Hollister said as he wrapped a tennis racket for a young man. The customer looked down at little Sue and said, "Do you mean the ones that were on television last night? Those Indians are in the Pioneer Village in Foxboro."

"That's right!" Sue piped. "Patchy would have lots of friends there."

After the customer had left, Mr. Hollister telephoned to Foxboro. The director of Pioneer Village told him that the museum would gladly accept a wooden Indian as a gift.

"Ask him how The Settlers' Friend is," Sue begged her father.

Mr. Hollister inquired about the statue and was told it was on exhibit.

"Fine," Mr. Hollister said. "We may bring you another one—that is, if my children agree," he added. "After all, it's their Indian."

Sue ran outside to tell the others what had happened.

"Good idea!" Pam declared.

"I'll vote yes," Pete said, "if it's okay with Dave."

"Oh, goody!" Holly declared. "When Snow Flower comes, we can all take Patchy with us to the Pioneer Village!"

Holly glanced around to tell Ricky. By now the crowd had thinned out, and she saw her brother standing several feet from the wooden Indian, waving a lasso. When the loop was large enough, Ricky flung it over Patchy's head. He gave what he thought was a little tug. But it was strong enough to make the heavy statue teeter.

"Yikes!" Ricky cried. "It's falling!"

CHAPTER 4

A WHISTLE-PIGGY BANK

PETE and Pam rushed to the falling Indian, and a couple of grownups did the same. Together they pushed the wooden figure back into place.

"I'm sorry," Ricky said, hanging his head. "Old Patchy could have gotten awful banged up on account of what I did."

Hearing the commotion, Mr. Hollister had come from the store in time to see the statue rescued. "I think our Indian would be safer at home," he said. "We've had enough advertising for one day at The Trading Post."

"Oh, good!" Pam said. "Can we take him back in the truck, Daddy?"

Her father said yes, and called Indy, who drove the pickup to the front of the store. Pete and Mr. Hollister loaded Patchy into the back, rifle and all. Then the children climbed in with him. When they reached the Hollister home, Holly and Pam insisted that the wooden Indian be brought inside.

"The living room would be the safest place for him," Pam said.

"Yes. Then we can keep Patchy company all evening," declared Holly.

With everyone helping, the Hollisters' treasure was carried inside and placed near the grandfather clock in the living room. The children thanked Indy, and as he left, Pete hurried to the phone to call Dave.

When Mrs. Hollister came downstairs to see what was going on, she smiled and said, "Well, children, do we have a permanent guest in our home?"

"Oh, no, Mommy," Holly spoke up. "Patchy is going to live at the Pioneer Village with the other wooden Indians."

"If Dave agrees," Pam reminded her.

"Yikes," said Ricky. "I hope he says no."

"He said yes," announced Pete a few minutes later.

"That's fine," remarked Mrs. Hollister. "I thought perhaps you would build a teepee for Patchy if he stayed here."

That evening Indy Roades phoned the Hollisters and told Pam that his sister Snow Flower would arrive on the noon plane next day.

"She thought Sunday would be a good time to get here, since we plan to leave for Foxboro on Monday," Indy added.

"May we pick her up, please?" Pam asked. Indy agreed.

Prospects of another adventure awakened all the children early next morning. Holly was first one down the stairs. Reaching the bottom, she screamed.

"Oh, dear, what's wrong?" Pam asked as she hastened down the carpeted steps.

Holly clapped one hand over her mouth. With the other she pointed at the wooden Indian's head. Draped on top of it was White Nose, the cat! She was bent far over, peering into the Indian's face.

"White Nose, get down or you'll tickle Patchy and he'll sneeze!" Holly giggled in delight.

As the others came trooping down, White Nose leaped to the floor and went off to her kittens in the basement. The youngsters' faces were shining as they dressed for church, and when they returned, Mrs. Hollister drove her excited children to the airport.

They arrived in their station wagon ten minutes before Snow Flower's flight was due. This gave them time to reach the observation deck and watch for the jet plane to come in.

"There it is now!" Pete said as the huge aircraft touched down on the runway and taxied up to the main building.

Soon the passengers began to stream from the airplane. Six pairs of eyes roamed over every person who got off.

"Yikes, Mother!" Ricky said. "I don't see Snow Flower!"

"Neither do I," Pam said.

Finally the last person walked into the airport

building. The downcast children looked at their mother.

"Crickets, she didn't come," Pete said. "Now we can't go to Foxboro."

"There may be some mistake," Mrs. Hollister replied. "Did Indy tell you what his sister looks like?"

Ricky spoke up. "She looks like an Indian, of course!"

"Now, there's where we may be wrong," Mrs. Hollister said. "Let's hurry to the waiting room."

The youngsters scurried down from the observation deck into the big airport building and walked across it, glancing this way and that at the passengers.

"What a goose I am!" Pam thought as she scanned the faces of the men and women. "Emmy Roades doesn't have to wear Indian clothes!"

As Mrs. Hollister sighed and looked about, a pretty, dark-haired woman dressed in the latest fashion approached her. "Excuse me," she said with a pleasant smile. "Are *you* Mrs. Hollister?"

"Why, yes—and you're Snow Flower!"

"Yes, I am, and I'm so pleased to meet you," Indy's sister said. Then, with a wink at Pam, she added, "Did you expect to meet an Indian with feathers?"

Noting the children's sheepish looks, she burst into a jolly laugh and put an arm about Holly and Sue. "I understand we're going to have a big ad-

"Did you expect an Indian with feathers?"

venture," she said. "My brother telephoned me all about the wooden Indians."

The Hollisters liked Emmy Roades instantly. She got into the front seat of the car with Mrs. Hollister, removed a pert hat and fluffed her short jet-black hair. "I'm so glad to be here," she said. "I haven't seen Indy in several years."

"You're coming directly to our house for dinner," Mrs. Hollister said. "And your brother will be there!"

On the way from the airport the youngsters took turns telling Emmy all that had happened in the last few days. Pete asked if the visitor had read about the train robbery. She had. Pam wanted to know if their guest knew something of wooden Indians. She did.

"How about dogs? Do you know anything about black cocker spaniels?" Holly asked as her mother drove steadily along.

When Emmy said that she once had a cocker spaniel, Holly was delighted. "Then you can help Indy's dog Blackie to be happy again," she said.

"I'll do my best," the Indian girl said with a smile. "I hear that Blackie misses his little whistle-pig."

"His whistle-what?"

"Whistle-pig. That's a nickname for a woodchuck or a ground hog," Emmy said, turning about in her seat. "Haven't you ever heard that before?"

The youngsters admitted that they had not, and

Emmy continued, "If we can find another whistle-pig for Blackie, I'm sure he'll stop moping around."

Now Indy's sister was firmly their friend. Mrs. Hollister admired her, too. "Your outfit is so fashionable," she complimented the Western woman.

Emmy told them why. She was a dress buyer for the largest department store in Phoenix, Arizona. "I love clothes," she said. "I like to buy and sell them."

Ricky leaned over the back of the seat, his chin resting in his hands. "And we thought you'd be wearing a fringed buckskin jacket!" he said with a sigh.

When they arrived at the Hollisters' home, Indy came out to the car to greet Emmy. The children beamed as brother and sister hugged each other. Then everyone trooped happily into the house.

Mrs. Hollister and Pam went straight to the kitchen for last-minute dinner preparations. While Emmy was admiring Patchy, Sue busied herself in her bedroom. Later, as her mother called everyone to the table, the little girl came down the stairs crying, "Look what I have! A whistle-piggy bank!"

Sue held up a pink china pig. In its snout she had inserted a small whistle. Blowing on it, she skipped to the table. "Blackie will be happy when he sees this," she said.

They all laughed, then took their seats. After Pam said grace, everyone enjoyed the delicious meal. They had almost finished the chocolate-cream-pie dessert when Mrs. Hollister cocked her head and said, "Have you children ever heard the woodchuck tongue-twister?"

The youngsters said they had not.

"Well, here it is," their mother replied and recited:

"If a woodchuck would chuck
All the wood a woodchuck could chuck
How much wood would a
Woodchuck chuck
If a woodchuck could chuck wood?"

"Yikes! When did you learn that?" Ricky asked, looking very pleased at his mother.

"When I was your age," she said. "My grandfather taught me. Let's hear you say it."

The children repeated it slowly and their mother teased, "Oh, come now, *faster*." Then the racket began as each child tried to outdo the other in racing through the tongue-twister.

Everyone had a jolly time and all the Hollisters were sorry when Emmy left with her brother to spend the night at his house. She took the whistle-piggy bank with her and promised to see if Blackie would respond. Next morning when she and Indy returned, Emmy reported sadly that the cocker spaniel did not believe the piggy bank was a real ground hog.

"He's smart, that's why," said Sue, as she took her bank.

"Blackie's out in the car," Emmy went on, "just in case we see a real, live whistle-pig on the way."

"Oh, goody!" Holly exclaimed, clapping her hands and jumping up and down.

It had been decided that the travelers would take the Hollisters' station wagon, so all the suitcases were loaded into it. Indy also put in a large carton of canned dog food and Blackie's water bowl. Then Emmy called the pet and he hopped into the back seat.

"Wait," said Pete. "I forgot something." He hurried into the house and returned with his pocket-size transistor radio. "You never can tell," he remarked. "This might come in handy."

As he spoke, Sue came out of the house carrying a brown paper bag.

"What do you have there?" Pam asked.

"It's a secret," replied the little girl, "and I'm going to take it along."

Now everything had been packed except for the wooden Indian.

"We'll tie him to the luggage rack on top of the car," Indy said.

"I'll get a cover for him," Pete offered and went into the garage. He took a plastic sheet from a shelf, and as he hurried out he gave Domingo a pat on the back. "We won't be gone too long, old boy," he said.

Mr. Hollister and Indy lifted Patchy, with his tomahawk and rifle, onto the top of the car.

When the wooden figure had been covered with the plastic and tied securely, Mrs. Hollister said, "Oh, goodness! It looks as if someone were hiding on the roof of our car with a gun! See how clearly it's outlined?"

"Oh, Mother!" Pete replied. "No one's going to notice!"

Mrs. Hollister looked doubtful, but said no more. She kissed her children good-by and they got into the station wagon. "Don't worry about them," Emmy said. "Indy and I will take good care of your family, Mrs. Hollister."

With the youngsters waving and calling good-by, the car backed out of the driveway and headed for New England. Sue sat on Emmy's lap, with Holly between her and the driver. The morning was crisp and clear. Soon Shoreham was left behind and the open road lay ahead.

But the car had gone no more than ten miles when suddenly the wailing sound of a siren was heard. Pete turned around and looked out the rear window. "A police car is after us!" he exclaimed.

CHAPTER 5

WHITE ELEPHANTS

"THAT policeman can't be chasing us!" Indy said, glancing at the speedometer. "We're not going too fast."

Nevertheless, the officer pulled alongside the station wagon and motioned it to the side of the highway.

"Oh, dear! We're going to be arrested!" Holly said, biting her lip.

"There's nothing to worry about," Emmy told her.

"Hello, there!" said the officer as he walked up to their car.

"Good morning," Indy said. "Is there something wrong?"

The officer glanced at the roof of the car. "It looks as if somebody were hiding under that cover with a gun in his hand," the policeman said. "What have you got up there?"

"A wooden Indian!" Ricky spoke up, and added, "Yikes! Mother was right!"

The police officer looked surprised. "Are all these children yours?" he said to Emmy.

"Oh, dear no!" she replied, and quickly told about their trip.

"Of course it's all right to carry the wooden Indian on top of your car," the policeman said, grinning. "But you'd better put the rifle inside."

"It's wooden, too," Pam explained.

"It looks pretty real," the officer said. "You might be stopped again."

Pete and Indy stepped out, removed the rifle and packed it in the back of the station wagon.

"All right," the policeman said finally. "Have a good trip!" As he was about to leave, Sue opened her paper bag, and pulled out the whistle-piggy bank. She blew it at the officer, then said, "This is a whistle-pig but it doesn't make Blackie feel better!"

The policeman gave a puzzled smile. After Holly had explained about the dog and the woodchuck, the officer reached inside the car, patted the spaniel's head and said, "You'll find lots of whistle-pigs where you're going. Blackie should be very happy."

As they continued on the trip, Pete pulled out his transistor radio and tuned in various stations along the way. The news broadcasts still told of the big search going on in New England for the train robbers.

Indy made a quick stop for lunch, and in the middle of the afternoon Ricky said, "I'm getting hungry again, Indy!"

"Me too!" said Pete.

Emmy smiled and said, "Let's have some ice cream." At the next roadside stand Indy pulled up and bought cones for everyone, including Blackie. Holly held the dog's ice cream for him, and he licked it as they rode along. Then he lay down again with his head on her lap.

"In an hour or so," Emmy said, "we'll look for a good restaurant. I want you children to be well fed."

Late in the afternoon Pam spied a sign by the roadside. It said: CHURCH SUPPER TONIGHT. ALL YOU CAN EAT. COME AND SEE THE QUILTING BEE.

"That sounds interesting," Emmy said. "Let's go there."

Sue looked worried. "I don't want to get stung," she said.

Pam chuckled. "A quilting bee is a kind of sewing party, honey," she explained.

The sign had said that the church supper was being held in the next town, and they had no trouble finding the place. The church sat back on a broad green lawn. In the front were several booths decorated with bright bunting. To one side was an outdoor kitchen. Near that were rows and rows of wooden tables and benches.

"Crickets!" Pete cried out. "We're just in time for the dinner!"

Indy pulled into a large parking lot and stopped two cars away from another station wagon which looked just like the Hollisters'.

"It'll be easy to find our car," Ricky said as they all stepped out. "Because there are two of them here together."

As Indy went to buy dinner tickets, Emmy and the children walked about the cool, tree-shaded lawn.

"Oh, look over there!" the Indian girl said. "They're having a white elephant sale!"

"What?" Sue said, glancing about. "I don't see any white elephants, Emmy."

"Neither do I," Holly spoke up.

"Oh, you sillies!" said Pam. "Haven't you ever heard of this kind of sale?"

When they said no, their sister explained that odds and ends which people kept in their homes and never used were called white elephants. Occasionally a church or civic group would hold a sale and everyone would contribute things they did not want to keep any more.

"It must be junk," said Ricky.

"Oh, you can find lots of nice things sometimes," Emmy replied. "Let's take a look."

They walked up to a long booth and Emmy gave each of the children a twenty-five-cent piece. "You can shop for bargains," she told them with a wink.

As the youngsters looked over a vast assortment of crockery and bric-a-brac, more people began to arrive for the supper. By the time Indy came with the tickets, the children had made their purchases.

"Now let's see what you all bought," Emmy said.

"I got a treasure!" declared Sue. In her chubby little fist she held a pin cushion in the shape of a mermaid.

Pete displayed an old-time police whistle. Pam had a hand-painted flower vase, and Holly a small statue of a bluebird.

"What did you get, Ricky?" Pete asked as his brother held his hand behind his back.

"Nothing fancy."

"Let's see it!" Holly begged.

"Aw, it's nothing girls would like."

"I'll bet it's a teensy wooden Indian," said Sue.

"No it isn't," Ricky said. From behind his back he brought a small black leather box.

"What's in there?" asked Emmy, looking curious. Ricky snapped open the top of the case. Inside lay six eye droppers of various sizes.

"Eye droppers!" Holly exclaimed. "What can you use those for?"

"What can you use your old bluebird for?" Ricky asked. Then he grinned and added, "You never know when you're going to need an eye dropper."

He snapped the lid shut, and the visitors found places at a long table spread with a white cloth. In a few moments, young people from the church began serving the diners.

Great, steaming platters of chicken and beef were placed on the table. Along with these were bowls of succotash, mashed potatoes, pickles, olives and celery. Then heaping trays of warm fresh bread

"Let's see it!" Holly begged.

were brought in and placed beside dishes of butter, jams and relishes.

Ricky glanced at Emmy. "May we start now?"

"Not yet," Holly whispered, "till we say grace."

"Yikes! This is a big meal! We should say a long grace, Pam!"

The older girl said a short one, however, and they all began to eat the delicious food. Blackie lay down at Indy's feet and waited patiently. Happy talk and laughter drifted over the tables as the townspeople enjoyed the fine meal.

A huge pitcher of milk placed before the children was soon empty and another quickly put in its place.

"Hurray!" Indy said finally. "Here comes the dessert!" It proved to be two kinds of pie, apple and blueberry.

"Gee whizzickers! Can I have a piece of each?" asked Ricky.

"You'll burst," Emmy warned him.

The red-haired boy only grinned as the waiter gave him a helping of each. When he had finished, Ricky heaved a large sigh.

"I'll be amazed if you can stand up," said Pam with a chuckle.

Ricky nodded in agreement. "I'd like to find a place to lie down," he said. "I feel kind of funny."

Emmy told him he might go back to the car, while the others watched the quilting bee which would follow.

Ricky's grin faded as he walked slowly toward the parking lot. Head down and feeling logy, the boy opened the door of the station wagon and flopped face down on the back seat. In a few minutes he was fast asleep. Indy and Pete, meanwhile, led Blackie over to the outdoor kitchen where a stout, pink-faced woman gave the dog a plate of chicken scraps and a bowl of milk.

"No charge," she said cheerfully.

While the spaniel ate, Emmy and the girls went to a table where the quilting bee had begun. Around it sat eight women sewing on one patchwork quilt.

"This is called a friendship quilt," said a tall, thin lady with gray hair. She explained that in olden days children wrote their names on the patches. "So you had your friends' autographs covering you when you went to sleep," the woman said, beaming at Pam.

"I'd like to make a friendship quilt some day," Pam told Emmy. "Maybe all the girls in our neighborhood could make one."

The church ladies bent to their task with their needles nipping in and out. Even tomboy Holly watched, fascinated, as rows of tiny stitches grew, criss-crossing the quilt.

"There's a nice warm layer of cotton material between the front and the back of this," the tall woman explained, "and we're sewing the three parts together."

The children watched a little longer, then Emmy

said, "I wonder how your brother Ricky is faring. Gracious! I never saw a boy eat so much!"

At that very moment Ricky's eyes fluttered open. As he came awake the boy suddenly realized that the station wagon was moving. In fact, it was bumping and joggling over a rough road.

Ricky sat up slowly. In the driver's seat was a woman he did not know!

At first the redhead was tongue-tied with fright. Then he blurted out, "Help! Where are you taking me?"

Startled, the driver jerked the wheel. The car swerved from the road and headed into a corn field!

CHAPTER 6

A SASSY GOOSE

FRIGHTENED by Ricky's outcry, the lady driver screamed as her car bounced into the corn field. The left front wheel hit a rock and *bang!*

The station wagon came to a halt and the woman turned around in her seat. "Goodness gracious! A boy!" she exclaimed. "How did you get into my car?"

"I—I thought it was ours," Ricky replied. "We have one just like it."

"Parked at the church supper?"

"Yes, ma'am."

"That's right. I saw it. Goodness gracious, I was afraid you were one of the robbers!"

"You mean the bandits who held up the train?" Ricky asked.

"Yes," the woman said, stepping out of the car to look at the damage.

Ricky, too, got out and looked at the left front wheel. "You have a flat tire," he said. "I'll change it for you."

The woman introduced herself as Mrs. Callie

55

Dorn. She had short curly gray hair and plump cheeks, still pink from excitement.

"I'm Ricky Hollister," the boy said as he got the tire tools from the back of the station wagon.

With Mrs. Dorn helping him, Ricky jacked up the station wagon and put the spare tire on the car.

"I think I'd better go back. They'll be looking for me," Ricky remarked, glancing along the country road.

"I'll take you, of course," Mrs. Dorn said. She thanked him for helping her, then started back toward the church. When they arrived, Ricky and Mrs. Dorn saw a crowd of people gathering about the Hollisters' station wagon.

The boy got out and ran toward them. "Here I am!" he called. "I got in the wrong car!"

Mrs. Dorn followed close behind him. "And nearly scared the wits out of me!" she said. "I'm surprised he got the cars mixed up, because yours has that funny-looking bundle on the roof and mine hasn't."

"I guess I was too full to notice," Ricky said sheepishly.

Emmy thanked Mrs. Dorn, and Indy offered to have the blown-out tire repaired.

"Thank you, but I'll take care of that," the woman said, adding that she was glad Ricky had not been one of the train robbers.

"It'll be growing dark soon," Emmy said. "We

must find a place to stay around here. Do you know of a motel, Mrs. Dorn?"

The woman replied that there was none for quite a few miles. "However, I take guests in my house," she said, "if you don't mind something old-fashioned but comfortable."

When it was agreed that they would stay at Mrs. Dorn's place, the travelers climbed into their station wagon and followed the woman down the same country lane where Ricky had given her a fright earlier in the evening.

The road wound up a hill. Near the top and to the left sat an old white farmhouse with lacy-looking columns lining the long porch. Indy drove to the back of the house and parked near Mrs. Dorn's car in front of a small barn.

As the children piled out of the station wagon, Blackie stood up and stretched, then lay down full length on the back seat and closed his eyes. No amount of coaxing could make him move.

"Let him alone," said Pete. "He wants to sleep in the car."

"Do you have any animals?" Holly asked the farm woman.

"I keep only a few chickens and an old goose," Mrs. Dorn replied. "Her name's Alphonse, but goodness knows why. She's not very friendly, I'm afraid."

"Maybe it's because she has a boy's name." Pam giggled.

Pete and Ricky helped Indy carry the bags inside the house, and Mrs. Dorn showed the guests to their rooms. Tall, old-fashioned windows reached nearly from floor to ceiling. The furnishings were worn, but well polished, and there were bright-colored rugs on the floors.

While Indy and his sister talked with Mrs. Dorn, the children hurried downstairs and out of doors to look around the farmyard. It was nearly dusk as Pete led the way to a chicken run beside the barn. Sue tagged along, holding Pam by the hand.

When they reached the chicken pen, Sue scooted off behind the barn. In a moment she came flying back, her eyes wide with fear. "Help!" Sue screamed. "She's going to get me!"

A second later the largest goose Pam had ever seen half ran, half flew around the corner of the barn. Hissing and craning its long neck forward, it chased the little girl. The other children were taken by surprise as Sue and Alphonse, the goose, flashed past them.

"Help! Help!" the child cried as she ran down a green slope.

Just then out of the farmhouse door raced Emmy. She kicked off her shoes and started after the big bird at top speed.

"Yikes! Look at her go!" exclaimed Ricky.

Emmy caught up with the goose just as it was about to nip Sue. With a backhand swish the Indian girl caught its thin neck. "Enough of this!"

Sue and Alphonse flashed past.

she said. Emmy gave Alphonse a spank and sent her scooting toward the barn again.

As the other children ran up to Sue and her rescuer, Pete looked at Emmy with admiration in his eyes. "You'd have made a great outfielder!" he told her.

Indy, who had joined them by now, grinned when he heard this. "I'll tell you a secret," he said. "My sister *is* an outfielder. She plays softball with the department store team."

Sue, whose black hair clung to her forehead in sweaty little ringlets, threw her arms around Emmy and said, "Thank you for saving me from the bad goosey!"

By now it had grown too dark to play outdoors and the children went with the grownups back to the farmhouse. No sooner were they inside, when Ricky said, "I'm hungry."

"You must have a hollow leg," Indy remarked.

Mrs. Dorn spoke up quickly. "Young boys are always hungry," she said. "How would you all like to have cookies and milk?"

They followed her into the kitchen, where an old-fashioned coal range sat on a stone hearth. The room was fragrant from a bowl of apples which adorned the center of the sturdy, round oak table.

The farm woman went to the pantry and returned with a bowlful of sugar cookies. Then she poured glasses of milk for her guests.

"Mrs. Dorn," said Ricky as he munched on a

cooky, "tell us about the train robbers. Were they around here?"

"We think so," came the reply. "The police said that there were several suspicious characters who passed through town. The officers even looked in my barn to see if anyone were hiding there."

"Maybe it was a false alarm," Indy said. "After all, you're pretty far from Foxboro."

"That's where we're going tomorrow," Pam volunteered. "We're taking a wooden Indian to the Pioneer Village."

Mrs. Dorn chuckled. "So," she said, "that's what's tied on top of your car!" Then she added, "You'll meet Mr. Edmund Marshall. He's the museum director and my cousin's husband. He'll be very glad to get your Indian. Edmund's always on the lookout for new exhibits. Lately he has been trying to buy an old covered bridge."

"There aren't many around any more," Indy said.

"Has he found one yet?" Ricky asked.

"Yes," replied Mrs. Dorn. "It's right in Foxboro."

"Will they dismantle the bridge and rebuild it on the museum grounds?" Pete asked.

"That's the plan," the woman replied, and explained that a land dispute was holding up the sale of the relic. Added to that, a severe storm last spring had flooded the Woosatch River and weakened the bridge foundation.

"Edmund fears that the span may be destroyed before it can be bought and carried to the museum," she said, shaking her head.

While Mrs. Dorn chatted with her guests, Sue fell asleep on Emmy's lap with a cooky in her hand.

"If you'll excuse us, Mrs. Dorn," Indy said, "I think we'd better go to bed."

Pete went to sleep wondering if any of the train robbers were really lurking about that part of the country. He was awakened early next morning by a rooster crowing. Pete rubbed his eyes sleepily, then roused Ricky. "Why don't we get dressed and look around the place?" he whispered.

The two boys put their clothes on quietly and tiptoed out into the carpeted hallway. There they saw Pam and Holly, fully dressed, going in the same direction.

When they arrived at the first floor, all four were surprised to find Mrs. Dorn in the kitchen.

"Good morning, children," she said brightly. "Gracious, you're early risers!"

"May we feed the chickens for you?" asked Pam.

"Of course. You'll find a sack of corn just inside the barn door. You may scatter some of it in the chicken run."

The children had noticed that the oven was lighted, and the wonderful aroma of baking cookies filled the kitchen. Holly wondered if Mrs. Dorn were making a batch especially for them. The woman looked at the girl and guessed what she was thinking.

"Yes, they're for you," she said kindly. "They'll be done soon and you can take them along on your trip."

"Ummm, that'll be yummy," declared Holly. Beaming, the children thanked their hostess and hurried off to feed the chickens.

Although the eastern sky was bright, the sun had not yet risen. Pete reached the barn door first and entered. In the gloom he saw the feed sack with a metal scoop next to it. Pete opened the bag and scooped out a measure of corn. Suddenly as he walked out of the barn, there was a loud hissing behind him.

"It's Alphonse again!" Pam cried out. Spilling the corn, Pete ran away with the big goose hard after him. But just then there came a loud barking. Blackie leaped from the car window and raced across the grass toward Alphonse.

"Yikes! Blackie feels better!" Ricky cried out. The spaniel's ears flopped in the breeze as he made a beeline for the sassy goose.

Seeing the dog, Alphonse veered off with Blackie yapping at her heels. The chase went up the hill behind the barn. But suddenly the spaniel stopped, raised a paw and sniffed the morning air. He forgot all about the goose, and Alphonse waddled off to safety.

As Blackie ran farther up the hillside, Pete went

back to the barn, got more corn and scattered it among the chickens. The four children watched them cluck and bob their heads as they pecked at their breakfast.

Now the horizon was pink and the edge of the sun peeked over a distant hillside.

"Say, where did the dog go?" Ricky asked.

"Here, Blackie, Blackie!" Holly called.

"There he is!" exclaimed Pam, pointing to a black plume near the top of the green hill.

"That's his tail, all right," Pete said.

"But where's the rest of him?" asked Holly.

All they could see was Blackie's happy tail waving back and forth like a flag.

CHAPTER 7

ZUZU

THE HOLLISTERS ran up the hill toward the cocker spaniel.

"Blackie, what are you doing?" Pam called out.

"He's digging a hole, that's what," freckle-nosed Ricky said.

"No, he's not," Pete corrected. "Blackie's halfway in a whistle-pig's burrow!"

"Oh, look over there!" exclaimed Holly. Thirty feet from the dog a ground hog poked his head out of another hole and whistled. "The whistle-pig's coming out his back door!" Holly cried delightedly.

Blackie heard the sound, too. He pulled his head out of the hole and raced toward the woodchuck. The little creature looked at the dog with beady eyes, then ducked back into his burrow. Blackie peered down into it for a few moments before trotting over to the Hollisters. There was a smudge of brown earth on his wet nose.

"Good boy," Pete said, bending down to pat the dog. "You see, there are other ground hogs in the world, Blackie!"

With the spaniel frisking around their feet, the

children trooped back to the house for breakfast. Sue laughed and clapped her hands when she heard about Blackie's adventure. While the travelers ate bacon and eggs at the kitchen table, Mrs. Dorn told them more about ground hogs.

"They're really ground squirrels," she said. "When tourists see a roly-poly whistle-pig run across the road, they're liable to think that it's a beaver, a raccoon, or even a bear cub."

"Did you ever see a baby woodchuck?" Holly asked her.

"Yes," was the reply. "At first they're only four inches long—little blind pink things with no hair."

"Where are they born?" Pam asked.

"Underground, in grass-lined nests."

"When?" Pete spoke up.

"In the spring. About five woodchuck kits are born in a litter," the woman went on. "After they have grown some, each kit builds its own little burrow. Then, by September or October, they're ready for a four or five months' snooze."

The youngsters were surprised to hear that whistle-pigs hibernate like bears.

"What do they like to eat?" Ricky asked.

"Almost anything that grows, especially my garden vegetables," Mrs. Dorn said with a smile. "But they like oatmeal and bread, too," she added.

By the time her guests had finished breakfast, the farm woman had told them many facts about the creatures.

66

"You know a lot about woodchucks, don't you, Mrs. Dorn?" Pam said.

"Oh, yes. I think they're cute." Then she told them that the Algonquian Indians had a funny word for ground hog. "They called it *We-jack*."

"That's where we get our word woodchuck, I'll bet," Pete remarked.

"You're right," replied the woman. "And the Chippewas called it *kuk-wah-geeser*."

"I like the little geesers too," declared Sue.

"The French Canadians," their hostess went on, "named it the *siffleur*—the whistler."

The children wanted to ask more questions about the animals, but Emmy reminded them that it was time to leave.

While suitcases were being loaded into the car, Holly stayed in the kitchen with Mrs. Dorn and gave Blackie a bowl of milk for his breakfast.

When all the travelers were ready to get into the station wagon the farm woman handed Pam the package of cookies. Everyone thanked her and Sue gave her a big hug.

"Give my best to Edmund," Mrs. Dorn said and they promised they would.

Blackie was the last one to jump into the car. As it drove off, he looked back longingly at the field where he had played hide-and-seek with the whistle-pig.

All morning Indy and his sister took turns driving while the Hollisters played guessing games and munched cookies. As they neared the town of Fox-boro, Indy stopped the car at a roadblock where two policemen stood. One of the officers walked over and explained that this was part of the cordon drawn around the area to catch the train robbers.

"Do you think they're still here?" Pete asked.

"We believe two of them are," was the reply. "Four men held up the train. One pair escaped. The others are probably lying low, waiting for a chance to get away."

"We'll keep our eyes open for them," Ricky declared.

The officer chuckled. "Don't you worry about it, sonny," he said. "Pass on, and have a good time."

Five minutes later a large sign loomed up beside the road. RIDE THE CHAIR LIFT it said. SEE THREE STATES FROM THE TOP OF MOUNT WHITEHALL.

A mile later the travelers passed the entrance to the chair lift and saw the cables stretched up the steep slope of the mountain.

"Let's go for a ride!" Ricky suggested.

"Not now," Pete said. "We ought to see Fox-boro first."

The others agreed this would be a better idea.

After a few more miles, they arrived at Foxboro. It was a small New England town with neat white houses and big shade trees. Near the center of it, they saw the entrance to the Pioneer Village. Indy turned left into the spacious grounds and pulled

68

up at a ticket booth. On it was a sign, NO DOGS ALLOWED.

After paying admission, Indy drove the car into the nearby parking area and everyone got out, including Blackie. Pete let him frisk around for a few minutes, then put him back into the car. Sadly the dog stood on the seat and watched his friends walk through a big white gate into the Pioneer Village.

"Crickets, this is keen!" Pete said as they passed several quaint old shops. In the distance on a hill was a church with a tall steeple, and here and there were other knolls with houses on them.

As the visitors walked along the dirt road, they saw a wagon coming, drawn by two oxen. The driver was an old gentleman with a flowing beard, and behind him in the cart stood a dozen sightseers.

"I want to ride in the wagon!" Holly clamored.

"Me too!" Ricky exclaimed.

"We'll all go," Indy said and the children raced ahead calling to the driver. He stopped and the seven climbed into the back of the ox cart.

"Giddap!" the driver said, and the big beasts lumbered along.

Ricky made his way to the front of the wagon. "Please, may I learn to drive the oxen?" he asked, looking up at the bearded man.

The old gentleman reached over and pulled

Ricky onto the seat beside him. He put the reins in the lad's hands.

"Don't expect them to gallop," he said, chuckling. Then he warned the boy never to whistle to the animals. "This pair'll get balky if you do," he said.

For a short time the man showed Ricky how to handle the reins. Then the driver took over once more as the oxen started to plod up a little hill.

"Look, here's the Stagecoach Inn!" Pam called out as they reached the top and pulled up in front of a big white clapboard house with a long porch across the front.

"Hey, what are those men doing?" Ricky asked. He jumped down off the ox cart and the other children did the same, followed by Indy and Emmy. All hurried over to some men who were carrying wooden Indians out of the Stagecoach Inn.

"Look! There's The Settlers' Friend!" Pam exclaimed.

"Why are you moving the Indians?" Pete asked one of the men.

"We're going to shoot pictures for a national magazine."

"Where is Mr. Marshall?" Pete asked.

"There he is, helping us," the man answered, smiling. Pete and Pam hurried over to the museum director and introduced themselves. He was a square-shouldered man with sandy, graying hair. He was

"Don't expect them to gallop."

happy to hear that they had enjoyed their stay at Mrs. Dorn's place.

Holly spoke up, "Did you get your covered bridge yet, Mr. Marshall?"

"So you heard about that, eh? No, but we're trying."

Then Pete quickly told about the Indian they had brought along.

Mr. Marshall called one of his helpers and they went with the boys and Indy to the parking lot to get Patchy. Together they carried him to the front porch of the Stagecoach Inn. How fierce he looked beside the other friendlier Indian faces!

"He's an unusual specimen," Mr. Marshall said, beaming. "I am grateful to you children for giving your Indian to the museum. All of you may come to see him as often as you like," he added. "I'll leave word at the gate to let you in free."

The travelers thanked him. Then, as the photographer prepared to take the pictures, Indy said, "We'd better go now. We have to find a motel."

They located one not far from the museum. It had a good view, overlooking the town. Emmy signed for four rooms, which were all in a row with connecting doors.

While Pete and Pam helped Indy and Emmy with the luggage, Ricky, Holly and Sue played hide-and-seek, with Blackie tagging at their heels. They raced from room to room. Finally, in the one that was to be Ricky and Pete's, the redhead slammed the door. Instantly there were three loud raps at the outside entrance.

"I'll bet that's the manager," Holly said. At once the three children dived under the bed.

"Maybe he won't let us stay here because we're too noisy," Holly whispered.

"Hey, what's this?" Ricky said, looking up at the box spring. Pinned to it was a piece of folded paper. He took it off and opened it. On the paper was a map, drawn in pencil.

Just then a voice called out, "Open the door, please! I have the suitcases!"

"That's Pete!" Holly exclaimed and wriggled from under the bed to let her brother in. He set the baggage down.

"Look what we found," Ricky said, holding out the map.

Pete studied it. "Crickets! This shows the outskirts of Foxboro where the railroad crosses the Woosatch River. Maybe this has to do with the robbery!" The other children followed Pete as he hastened to Pam and the grownups.

They, too, were excited when they saw the map. Then all hurried to the motel clerk. "Say, this is the best clue yet," the man declared, and quickly telephoned the police. Two men in a patrol car arrived minutes later.

"That was a great piece of detective work," one of the officers told Ricky.

"But it was only by accident," said Holly honestly.

None the less, the policemen said that they were bright children to recognize the map as a clue.

"We'll check immediately," one of the officers added, "to see who has occupied that room in the last few weeks."

"Crickets!" Pete exclaimed. "We're into the middle of the mystery already."

Indy shook his head. "You Hollisters seem to attract mysteries. It beats me!"

The travelers ate lunch at a restaurant connected with the motel. Then Pam remembered the Culver family. "Let's go see them now," she suggested.

The motel man gave them directions to the Culvers' house. It was quite near, two doors down the street past the general store and across from the museum grounds. "You don't need me then," said Emmy. "I'll stay here with Blackie and write letters." Indy also asked to be excused, saying he wanted to take the car to the service station, so the children set off alone.

When they came to the house, they saw a little girl sitting on the front steps. She had straight blond hair which hung to her shoulders, and big brown eyes.

"We're looking for the Culvers," Pam said, walking up to her.

74

"I'm Azuba Culver," the child told her.

Sue dimpled. "Zuzu!" she exclaimed. "I like that name!"

The little girl laughed and wrinkled her sunburned nose. "Nobody's called me Zuzu before," she said, "but you may if you want. It's no worse than Azuba."

"I think it's better," said Ricky.

Just then an attractive woman came to the door. Pam explained who they were.

"Oh, yes. Do come in," Mrs. Culver said warmly. "I got a letter from Mrs. Mead this morning, saying that you would be here."

Pete, Pam and Sue went into the house with the woman. But Holly and Ricky stayed to talk with Zuzu.

"Would you like to see my playhouse?" the little girl asked them. "My sisters are in there now."

"Oh, yes!" Holly replied.

"And we can have some ice cream, too," their new acquaintance added. The three children walked into the backyard. Several trees shaded the lawn and part of the flower garden. Toward the back was a small playhouse.

"I'll show you my sisters," Zuzu said, grasping Holly's hand. When they got to the playhouse, the Culver girl walked in with Holly close behind. Ricky followed.

"We have visitors," Zuzu said brightly.

Holly stared. "Are *those* your sisters?"

75

CHAPTER 8

THE EAR-WIGGLER

SEATED on two small chairs were the oddest-looking dolls Ricky and Holly had ever seen. They were really milk bottles dressed in long skirts and shawls, with kerchiefs over their "heads."

Zuzu stood there, rocking back and forth on her heels. "Their names are Laura and Jane," she said proudly.

"But—but they're only 'magination sisters," Holly blurted.

"That's right," Zuzu answered brightly. "I have lots of 'magination things."

Ricky looked at her from the corner of his eyes. "What about the ice cream?" he asked.

"Here it is!" Zuzu said, stepping over to a small table. On it sat a small pan full of gooky mud.

"That's my 'maginary ice cream," she explained. "Will you have some?"

"Ugh!" Ricky said, but Holly was kinder. She went over and made believe she was tasting some of the mud ice cream. "Mmm, it's delicious!" Then she picked up the dolls and hugged them.

By this time the other children had finished

talking with Zuzu's mother and had walked back to the garden playhouse.

Seeing them, Holly quickly ran out and whispered to Pam about Zuzu's queer dolls.

"Oh, yes," the older girl said softly. "Her mother told us about that. Sometimes it's hard to know whether Zuzu really means things or not."

After Pam and Sue had pretended to taste some of the make-believe ice cream, Pete said, "Why don't we go to the general store and get real ice cream cones?"

"Oh, good!" Zuzu exclaimed. "I want chocolate."

"Let's get double-dips," Ricky said. "Come on, I'll race you, Holly!" In a few minutes he and his sister pounded up the wooden steps onto the porch of the store. The others were close behind.

When Holly opened the door a little bell tinkled. "Mmm," she said as she walked in, "this smells yummy—like penny candy."

"What a nice old-fashioned store," said Pam. On one side of the large room was a long counter, and in the middle of the floor stood a black pot-bellied stove.

"Crickets," exclaimed Pete. "Look at that big iron monster!"

From somewhere came a chuckle and a deep voice said, "It may look like a monster now, but it's a warm cheerful friend in the winter."

The children looked around. At the far end of

77

the counter they saw a tall, thin, blond man seated on a high stool. As he got up and walked toward them, he smiled.

"What may I get for you?" he asked.

"We'd like ice cream cones," Pete replied. The storekeeper led the way to a soda fountain on the other side of the store. As the visitors gave their orders, he scooped out big double-dips of luscious ice cream. "And I know what Azuba wants," the man said. "She likes chocolate."

While the youngsters licked the ice cream cones they explored the country store. The Hollisters had never seen one exactly like it before. The walls were covered with shelves of merchandise and on one of the counters lay bolts of bright-colored cloth. In a corner of the room was an alcove marked "Post Office."

"Crickets," Pete thought. "This store has everything."

The girls and Ricky were gathered around a glass case filled with many kinds of candy—including licorice, candy dots on long strips of paper, lollipops and homemade fudge bars.

After the others had made their choices, Pam asked, "Would you like some candy, Zuzu?"

The child nodded and pointed to a small pailful of licorice whips. The storekeeper reached in and got several for her.

Pam smiled and said, "You have so many good things, Mr.—"

"Wallace. My name is Mr. Wallace," the blond man told her. As he put the licorice into a bag, a handsome boy about Pete's age came in from a back room. He walked over casually to where Pete was examining the pot-bellied stove. "Hi."

"Hi."

"My name's Wally Wallace," the boy said.

"I'm Pete Hollister from Shoreham."

As Pete introduced his brother and sisters, they began to giggle and Sue said, "Walla Walla, you're funny!"

"Yikes!" Ricky burst out. "Wally can wiggle his ears!"

The New England boy grinned broadly and said, "I wondered whether you'd notice that!"

"Do it again," Holly begged.

Wally Wallace stood perfectly still and moved his ears up and down.

"Crickets, that's great!" Pete exclaimed. "I wish I could do that!"

"You ever try it?"

"No."

"It's easy. You just wiggle 'em, that's all."

The Hollister children, and even Zuzu, stood still and made all kinds of faces trying to make their ears move.

"Your left ear is going great," the new boy told Ricky. Everyone laughed to see this, even Wally's father, the storekeeper.

By this time Wally Wallace was a great favorite

"Wally can wiggle his ears!"

with the newcomers, and Pete said he was glad he had found a boy his age to play with in Foxboro.

"I like Walla Walla, too," Sue declared.

"Maybe I can show you around town, and the museum too," Wally offered. "I do odd jobs for Mr. Marshall, so he lets me come whenever I want."

"That would be neat," Pete said.

"Do you see anything more you want to buy?" Wally asked. Pam had been admiring two handmade quilts hanging on the wall.

"I'd love to get one of these for Mother," she said, "but I guess they're too expensive."

"They do cost a lot," the boy replied. "Why don't you give her some handmade soap?" He showed Pam a basket filled with small balls wrapped in colored tissue paper. She picked up one and sniffed it. "Umm, it smells spicy," she said, and bought a half dozen of them.

As Mr. Wallace wrapped the soap, he told her that there were many beautiful old quilts in the museum. "You ought to go see them," he said.

"Why don't you come there with us now?" Pete asked Wally.

The boy nodded and Pam said, "We have to take Zuzu home first."

On the way back, Zuzu said brightly, "I saw the robbers!"

"The train robbers?" asked Ricky.

The little girl bobbed her head up and down. "Near the old mill—that's where I saw them."

Pete winked at Pam, and Wally gave the girl a knowing glance. "You certainly do have a good 'magination," Ricky said, keeping a straight face.

"You'd better be careful what you tell us, Zuzu," Holly warned, "'cause we're detectives."

Zuzu's eyes grew round. "Oh," she said, "that's what I want to be."

By the time they came to Zuzu's house, the little girl's mouth was black in the corners from eating the licorice. She smiled sweetly, thanked them for the ice cream and candy, then skipped inside.

Wally and the Hollisters walked the short distance to the museum grounds. At the gate, Pete gave the attendant their names and he waved them in. As they approached the Stagecoach Inn, Pete and Pam told their new friend all about the wooden Indian and the chore they had come to do.

"Then let's measure The Settlers' Friend right away," Wally suggested. The children trooped into the old building, where they were greeted by a woman guide wearing an old-fashioned dress and sunbonnet. Wally asked her for a tape measure. She happened to have one in her purse and gave it to him.

"Thank you," Pam said. "We're going to measure an Indian." Wally led them to the long hall where the wooden figures stood in two rows, facing each other. Holly ran ahead and was first to reach The Settlers' Friend. "Here it is!" she called, and spun around, her braids slapping the side of the Indian.

But there they stuck!

"Oh, help!" Holly cried, trying to pull her head away.

Just then the woman guide hurried in and said, "Oh, dear, I should have warned you! I just remembered that The Settlers' Friend was given a coat of shellac this morning."

"Yikes, I can see that!" Ricky said, chuckling. "My sister's stuck!"

The kindly woman helped Pam to pull Holly's braids free of the Indian. But even then, several of her hairs stuck to the statue.

The woman hastened off to the basement and returned with a rag which had been dipped in alcohol. "It's not exactly French perfume," she said, "but it will get the stickum out of your hair." After Pam and Holly had thanked her, she said, "Come back tomorrow to measure the Indian. He'll be dry then."

"How would you like to see some old toys?" Wally asked as the children left the Stagecoach Inn. "Some of them are really ancient!"

The boy led the visitors into a building which looked like his father's general store. But instead of items for sale, there were shelves and tables of antique toys which had been found in homes around Foxboro.

The room was filled with a tinkling tune played by a small music box with a toy clown dancing on top.

On the shelf near it, Ricky spotted an old-time, horse-drawn fire engine, and Pete found an odd mechanical monkey. It was wearing a plumed hat, colonial coat, and carrying a drum.

A smiling woman attendant stepped over and wound up the toy. Fascinated, the boys watched the monkey stiffly beat the drum.

Meanwhile the girls admired the antique dolls. Many of them were dressed like ladies, and had lovely china heads. "Oh, they're so beautiful," Sue said.

"Yes," remarked Pam, "but I guess you had to be awfully careful or they'd break."

"Oh, look at these little cowbells," Holly said.

"They're kitty cowbells," Wally told them. "And they really ring, too."

Holly tinkled the bells and said, "Oh, I wish we could buy one of these for White Nose!"

"You may," said the friendly lady guide as she approached the girls. "At our souvenir shop there are some modern ones which the local people make."

After looking at all the toys, the children found the little gift store near the exit. Holly tried out several of the new kitty cowbells and bought one for White Nose, her pet cat in Shoreham.

Then Pam asked the saleswoman where the

quilts were displayed, and she was directed to a stone house next door. Pam, Sue, and Holly left the boys and went to see the counterpanes.

"Oh, aren't they beautiful!" Pam exclaimed as she admired the colorful bedcovers. They were stretched out full length in standing frames which the visitors could turn like the pages of a book.

Another woman attendant approached them and said, "Here is a quilt which I think you'd like, girls." She pointed to an ornate and faded coverlet made up of many squares. And in the middle of each one was a signature in ink.

"That's a friendship quilt," the woman said.

"We saw them making one," Pam told her.

"Oh, look!" Holly exclaimed, pointing to an odd name. "Cuz Phoebe!"

"Wouldn't it be nice to have a cousin Phoebe?" asked Pam. The girls examined the quilt in detail, noting a checkerboard on one patch, a table and flowers on another, an anchor, a chicken and even a tiger.

The boys, meanwhile, had walked across a large quadrangle toward a barn which Wally told them was filled with old-fashioned tools and farm equipment. In front of it, on a small rise of ground, stood two big wheels with nothing but an axle between them.

"Yikes!" Ricky said. "What's that, Wally?"

The Foxboro boy replied that the strange contraption had been used to roll timber down from

85

the hills. He explained that a large log was put over the axle and wheeled to the logging road, where it was loaded onto a horse-drawn wagon.

As the boys stopped and looked up at the old logroller, four other boys raced over to examine it. They were followed at a distance by a man and woman.

"What wild kids!" Ricky said as the boys pulled and tugged at the wheels. Even though the iron rims had sunk several inches into the ground, the newcomers rocked them loose.

The two grownups were talking and did not notice. In a few moments the wheels were pulled out of their resting place.

"Stop!" Pete yelled, but too late. The four lads ran off and the huge contraption began to roll down the hill directly toward him. In his haste to escape, Pete tripped and fell in the path of the giant wheels.

CHAPTER 9

A DANGEROUS BRIDGE

WHILE Pete scrambled to get out of the way, Wally and Ricky dashed toward the two huge wheels. They gave one a hard shove, changing the course of the old logroller. It missed Pete by inches, and crashed into a hitching post before it stopped.

The post, however, was so firmly imbedded in concrete that it did not move.

"Yikes," said Ricky, looking pale.

"No harm done, I guess," Pete said, and slapped Wally on the back. "Thanks for saving me. That was close!"

Wally grinned, then helped Pete and Ricky try to push the wheels back to their starting place. As they did, Mr. Marshall came out of the Stagecoach Inn.

"Don't play with that logroller, boys!" he called, hurrying over to help them. Wally quickly told him what had happened. The museum director looked about for the four boys who had caused the mischief, but they were out of sight.

"Everything seems to go wrong today," Mr.

Marshall said, glancing skeptically at the sky. A worried frown crossed his forehead.

"Did something happen?" Pete asked.

"Not yet," came the reply. Mr. Marshall said that the weatherman had predicted a storm. "One of those hurricanes is on its way here. Hurricane Cora, I think is what they call it. And if it hits us hard, I'm afraid that old bridge'll be washed out this time."

As he spoke, Pam, Holly and Sue joined them.

"Why do they name hurricanes after girls?" Sue piped up.

The sudden question derailed the conversation for a moment. Nobody seemed to know the answer. But finally Ricky grinned and said, "I know why they're named after girls. Who ever heard of a *he*-ricane?"

Even Mr. Marshall smiled for a moment, then looked worried again. At Pam's request he began to tell the story of the dispute over the wooden bridge. A maiden lady named Patience Jones had owned the span and the land at each end of it. In her will she left the property to a grandniece.

"You mean a little girl?" Holly asked.

"No, the grandniece is a middle-aged woman herself," the man went on. "She is willing to sell the bridge. But a grandnephew, who lives in France, has said that the will is not a good one."

The museum man explained that the grand-nephew challenged the signature of Patience Jones, saying that it was a fake.

"It should be easy to check," Pete spoke up. "Aren't there any authentic signatures to compare it with?"

"That's the problem," the man replied. "We can find no other signature of the Jones woman."

Suddenly Pam's eyes lit up. "I know what!" she exclaimed. "Maybe she signed a friendship quilt!"

"We've thought of that," Mr. Marshall said, shaking his head. "But we haven't been able to locate one with her name on it." He added that if the signature could be found, it would settle the case once and for all. "We hope," he said, "that it'll prove the will is good, so we can buy the bridge."

"Then let's go search for other friendship quilts," Pam said. "Maybe we could find one signed by Patience Jones."

The museum director shrugged. "Even if you did, we couldn't buy and move the bridge before the hurricane hits," he said and added, "But if you want to look for a quilt, go ahead. Don't bother with those in the museum though. We've examined them all."

As the disappointed man walked off, Pete said, "Wally, just where is this covered bridge?"

"Not far from here—near the Old Mill Road. How would you like to go see it after supper tonight?"

"Great idea!" Pete declared. "Will you meet us at our motel?"

"Sure thing. I have to go now and do some errands for Dad." Wally wiggled his ears and ran off.

The Hollisters returned to the motel and told Indy and his sister all that had happened.

"Oh, Emmy!" Pam said. "If we could only find that signature. I feel sorry for Mr. Marshall." Then she added, "I wonder where Patience Jones lived. If she made a friendship quilt, it might still be somewhere in her house."

"Let's ask the motel clerk," Pete suggested.

"Good idea," Indy approved. "At the same time inquire about an extra-special good place to eat supper."

When Pete and Pam questioned the man at the desk, he smiled and said, "You can kill two birds with one stone by going to the Green Mountain Inn. It's an excellent restaurant, and is also the house where Patience Jones used to live." After he gave them directions to the place, the children thanked him and hurried back to the others.

Pete reported what the clerk had told them.

"Then let's go to dinner right away," Emmy said.

As they got into the station wagon, they noticed that the clear blue sky had changed to a dark, sullen gray.

"Looks as if the hurricane is approaching," Indy said.

"Pam," said Emmy, slipping an arm around the

girl's shoulders, "don't be disappointed if it turns out that you've wasted your time looking for a quilt. I'm afraid the bridge may not survive the storm."

"I know," said Pam, "but I'm going to try to find Patience Jones's signature anyway."

Ten minutes later Indy parked in front of a big white house set in the middle of a green lawn. As they walked in the front door, they were met by the hostess, a tall silvery-haired woman wearing a flowered dress.

"We're detectives!" Sue spoke up as the hostess led them to a table.

"Gracious!" she exclaimed. "And what do you expect to find here?"

As the visitors seated themselves, Pam explained their quest.

"It is likely that Patience Jones made a friendship quilt," the hostess said. "They were very popular. But we have none here." Then she introduced herself as Mrs. Hull. "I own this house," she explained with a smile. "The day before I bought it, all the furnishings were sold at auction. I looked them over, but I don't recall seeing a quilt."

"Maybe it was mixed up with other things," suggested Pam, "in a box or a chest."

Mrs. Hull thought for a moment, then nodded slowly.

"Now that you mention it," she said, "there was

one big carton of odds and ends which was sold without being opened."

"Do you remember who bought it?" Pam asked eagerly.

"Yes," came the reply, "it was—" Then the hostess stopped short. "Please excuse me," she said quickly. "Here comes another customer."

The children could hardly wait for the woman to return.

"Meantime, let's decide what we're going to eat," suggested Indy. While the others were studying the large menu cards, Sue wriggled down from her chair. She ran over to a huge fireplace at one end of the dining room.

Mrs. Hull and Sue returned to the table at the same time. Emmy gasped when she saw the little girl, and the hostess exclaimed, "My dear, where have you been?"

Sue's face was streaked with soot. She pointed to the fireplace and said, "I was looking up to see if I could see Santa Claus, and my hands got dirty."

"Then you touched your face, poor child," Emmy said.

"It's nothing to fuss about," the hostess declared. She took the little girl by the hand and led her off. Soon Mrs. Hull returned with Sue looking bright-faced and eager.

"We've already given our orders to the waitress," Pam said, and added quickly, "Will you

"I was looking for Santa Claus."

please tell us who bought the box of odds and ends?"

"It was Mrs. Willow," the woman replied. "She lives on Old Mill Road."

"We're going near there tonight," exclaimed Pete, "to the covered bridge!"

"Then you'll pass her house," said the hostess.

"Oh, let's stop to see Mrs. Willow—please, Indy," begged Pam.

Before he could answer, Mrs Hull spoke up. "It's no use, my dear. Mrs. Willow won't be home until tomorrow. She always spends Tuesday at her sister's house, fifty miles from here."

Pam's face fell.

"Never mind," said Pete. "We'll go look at the bridge with Wally, anyhow."

Ricky frowned. "Just looking's no fun. There's a jungle gym in the backyard of the motel. I'd rather play on that."

"So would I," spoke up Holly.

"Me too," said Sue.

"All right," Emmy agreed. "I'll stay home with you three and Blackie."

"And I'll drive the others to the bridge," said her brother.

Although the dinner was delicious, the children were eager for it to be over. As soon as Indy had paid the bill and Pam had thanked Mrs. Hull, they all hurried out to the car.

Shortly after they reached the motel, Wally arrived. Pam told him about the box Mrs. Willow had bought at the auction.

Wally shook his head. "She probably won't remember what was in it. She's pretty absent-minded. I'll show you where she lives," he added.

Following the Foxboro boy's directions, Indy headed the car out of town. Soon they turned to the right over a modern bridge, then right again onto a narrow road, which ran along the river.

A short distance up the bank, Wally pointed out a small boathouse. "That's where I keep my motorboat," he said. "If you like, I'll take you for a ride."

"Crickets, that'll be great," Pete exclaimed.

"But we can't go for a day or so," Wally went on, "because I painted the boat. It's still drying in my backyard." Just then he pointed to a white house on a slope to their left. "That's Mrs. Willow's place," he said quickly.

Moments later they passed an old stone mill on the other side of the road. The roof had fallen in and the building, half hidden by drooping willow trees, lay in ruins beside the stream.

A short distance farther on, Wally told Indy to turn right once more. They drove into a rutted lane overgrown with weeds. Before them loomed the old covered bridge. Indy stopped the car and they all got out. It was almost dark and fireflies were twinkling on and off. Pete led the way over to a sign which said: DANGER. TRAVEL AT YOUR OWN RISK.

"I guess no one would drive on it any more," Pete said.

"No, but we can cross it on foot," Wally said. "It's kind of spooky inside."

As the explorers walked onto the wooden structure, their footsteps sounded hollow. It smelled dank and rotten.

Wally, in the lead, pointed out a big hole in the floor. Through it, the swift water of the stream could be seen below. Finally they came out of the other end of the bridge. Indy eyed the old span and shook his head. "I doubt if this thing can last through a hurricane," he remarked.

"All the same," declared Pam, "I won't give up hope. I'm going to keep looking for Patience Jones's signature."

"We'd better hurry back," put in Pete. "It's just about dark."

As they re-entered the bridge, there was a sudden *swoosh* and several black shapes flew around their heads.

Pam let out a squeak of fright.

"Swallows," Wally explained.

"I want to get out of here quick," the girl said, "before one of those birds bumps into me."

She hurried on ahead, able to see only the dim patch of daylight at the far end of the covered bridge.

But in her haste Pam forgot about the hole. Suddenly the quiet was shattered by a shrill scream as Pam fell through and into the river below!

CHAPTER 10

THE THREE-TOED TREE TOAD

PAM hit the water with a splash. The fall knocked the breath out of her, and she struggled in the swirling stream. As Pam tried to swim to shore, Pete, Wally and Indy raced across the bridge and along the river bank in the half darkness.

"This way, Pam!" Pete cried, catching sight of her bobbing head. "Swim over here and we'll get you!"

Pam swallowed a mouthful of water and coughed as she tried desperately to reach shore. But the swift current carried her farther downstream. The two boys and Indy ran along, keeping abreast of the struggling girl.

They stumbled through marshes of cattails and banged their toes on hidden stones as the chase led them closer to the old mill.

A quiet eddy lay behind the big wooden wheel. Seeing this, Pete called out, "Try to grab the wheel, Pam!"

With Indy and Wally right behind him, Pete was first to reach the ruined building. The boy scrambled over a broken stone wall and climbed to the top of the wheel. Pam had finally reached the quiet waters and was clinging, exhausted, to the side of the wheel.

"Hang on! I'll get you!" Pete called. But as he tried to climb down the wooden blades, the mill wheel creaked and gave a sudden lurch. Pete was tossed headlong into the water beside his sister! Surfacing quickly, he put an arm around Pam and swam with her to shallow water. Together they waded ashore through a patch of reeds.

"Are you hurt?" asked Indy as he helped the drenched girl onto the bank.

Breathlessly, Pam replied, "No." She had only skinned her left knee in the fall through the old bridge.

"But you look pretty tuckered out," Indy said. "We'll get you home right away." He told the boys to remain there with Pam while he went for the car. Indy hastened off into the darkness and soon the children heard his steps quicken on the loose gravel at the side of the road. Then all was quiet.

"This spooky old mill makes the back of my neck creep," Pete whispered, as he shivered in his wet clothes.

"Shhh," Pam said softly. "I think I hear something!"

All three children listened intently. The only noise was the rushing of the river.

"It sounded like a thump," the girl said.

"Maybe something hit the mill wheel," Wally

reasoned, "probably a log carried down by the stream."

"This would be a great place for the crooks to hide out, wouldn't it?" remarked Pete, peering keenly toward the road for a sign of headlights.

"An awful damp spot, I'd think," Wally said, looking at the crumbling walls behind them.

"Do mills have cellars?" Pete asked.

"Search me," his friend replied, and added, "Look, here comes Indy now."

Two bright headlights stabbed through the darkness. Then the car was maneuvered so that the beams clearly showed the waiting children how to reach the road.

With teeth chattering, Pete and Pam climbed into the back seat while Wally slid over beside the driver.

The wind was rising when they reached the motel and dropped Wally off. "See you tomorrow," he called out as he hastened toward his home.

"Now hot showers for both of you," Indy said to the shivering pair. "Scoot!"

When Pam and Pete hurried into their rooms, they found them empty. "Emmy must be telling the others a story," Pam thought as she turned on the hot water. Fifteen minutes later she was warm and dry in her pajamas and robe. She rapped lightly on Pete's door. He, too, was ready and together they went to Emmy's room. What laughs and giggles they could hear inside!

As Pete opened the door and entered with Pam, Emmy was saying, "Do you hear those little peeping tree frogs?" She was sitting on the bed with the three younger Hollisters while Blackie slept on the floor.

The children listened against the rising wind, then bobbed their heads in answer to Emmy's question.

"Well, I know a jingle about a tree toad," the Indian girl told them. "I'll say it slowly, then you repeat after me." She smiled and began:

> "A tree toad loved a she-toad
> That lived up in a tree.
> She was a three-toed tree toad,
> But a two-toed toad was he."

Sue, in her pajamas, squirmed and giggled.

"Wait, there's more!" Emmy said, and went on:

> "The two-toed tree toad tried to win
> The she-toad's friendly nod
> For the two-toed tree toad loved the ground
> That the three-toed tree toad trod."

Emmy recited the verse slowly once more and all the children repeated it.

"Now say it faster and faster," she urged them. The noise and laughter that followed caused Blackie to wake up and bark. Then Indy popped his head into the room.

"What's the joke?" he asked with a big grin.

"A free toad loved a she-toad that lived up in a twee!" Holly said quickly.

The giggling started again, and Ricky laughed so hard that he rolled over twice on Emmy's bed. Finally Sue stopped laughing and let out a big sigh. Emmy picked her up, walked into Pam and Holly's room and tucked the little girl into bed. Sue sighed once more. "Three-toed twee toad," she said softly, closed her eyes, and went fast asleep.

When Emmy returned to the others, Pete, Pam and Indy told of their adventure at the old mill.

"Oh, I'm so glad you're safe!" the Indian woman said, giving Pam a hug.

That night the sound of the wind in the tree branches lulled the five youngsters to sleep. In the morning when they awakened, the sky was dark with low, speeding clouds. Pete flipped on his transistor radio in time to hear the weatherman say that Hurricane Cora was indeed on its way to New England.

The newscaster followed with a report that the local authorities were intensifying their search for the two train robbers believed to be hiding out in the Foxboro area.

Pete's thoughts drifted to the old mill, but he decided that the police probably had searched it.

At breakfast, the three girls and Emmy agreed to go to Mrs. Willow's house on Old Mill Road in hope of finding a friendship quilt signed by Patience Jones. Pete and Ricky volunteered to measure The

Settlers' Friend while Indy explored more of Pioneer Village.

"Blackie can stay right here in the motel," Pam said.

After giving the dog his breakfast, the girls set off for Old Mill Road with Emmy driving. Pam gave directions and before long they pulled up at the foot of Mrs. Willow's hill. In the back of her house they could see a barn and shed.

Emmy and the girls climbed a steep flight of wooden steps to the front door. There they turned an old-fashioned jangly bell and Mrs. Willow appeared. "She looks like anything but a willow tree," Pam thought.

The woman was almost as wide as the door. Her hair was bright gold and was twisted into a small topknot held firmly by a tortoise-shell comb.

After Emmy had introduced herself and the girls, Pam explained their mission. "We understand that you bought a box of odds and ends at the Jones auction," she said. "We were wondering if there was a friendship quilt in it."

"Now, let me see," the woman said slowly, and Pam held her breath. "I think there was."

"Hooray!" Sue cried.

"Oh, please, may we see it?" Pam asked.

"'Cause it might have an important name on it," Holly said, trying to act very grown up.

"Goodness, I don't know exactly where it is," Mrs. Willow told them, "but come right in." As she led the way into the living room, she explained that she collected antique quilts. "And I have trunks in the attic just full of them," she said, puffing after the short walk from the hall.

"Can you look through them right now?" Pam asked hopefully.

The plump woman started to nod, then stopped short. "Oh, dear no! I forgot!" she exclaimed quickly, and Pam's face fell. Mrs. Willow said that she had to visit a sick relative in Foxboro and that a taxi was calling for her shortly. "But I'll look for the quilt later," she promised.

Disappointed, Emmy and the girls returned to their car and drove back to town.

"Let's go to the museum and find the boys," Holly suggested, and the others agreed. But when they reached the Stagecoach Inn, they found only Mr. Marshall in the hall with the wooden Indians.

"The boys measured The Settlers' Friend and left to explore the Village," the museum man reported. "Why don't you visit our Carousel Room while you're here? It's on the third floor. There are many wonderful old merry-go-round animals up there."

As the girls climbed the wooden staircase, Holly looked glum and said, "I'll bet Pete and Ricky are having more fun than we are."

At that moment her brothers were in the Village blacksmith shop. When they came out they met Mr. Marshall.

"I've been looking for you," he said to the boys. "Would you like to do me a favor?"

"Of course," Pete replied.

Mr. Marshall told them that the ox-cart driver was going to be away for an hour or two that afternoon. Would Pete drive the wagon full of tourists?

"Crickets! I'd be glad to," the boy replied.

"I'll help him," offered Ricky. "I know all about driving the oxen."

They were told to meet Mr. Marshall at one o'clock in front of the old church.

"Wait'll Holly hears this!" Ricky exclaimed.

"You can tell her right away," said Mr. Marshall. "Miss Roades and your sisters are in the Stagecoach Inn."

Pete and Ricky found the girls admiring the gaily colored wooden animals collected from old-time carousels. A costumed woman attendant was telling about the figures.

"You see, there are giraffes and lions and zebras, too," she said. "But in later years, horses became the most popular."

"And maybe easier to catch, too," Sue piped up.

The guide laughed and quickly finished her talk. At once Pete and Ricky burst out with their news.

"I wish I'd been with you," Holly said as they went downstairs. Outside they met Indy and all went to a cafeteria on the museum grounds for lunch.

Afterward the girls set off with Emmy to see the

inside of an old-time schoolhouse, and the boys trotted away to meet the museum director. He was on time, waiting in front of the old church with the ox team. The cart was filled with tourists. "Drive them around slowly," Mr. Marshall said, "and don't let the oxen get balky."

The boys climbed up onto the high seat. Pete picked up the reins. "Giddap!" he called, and the big beasts lumbered off.

"Yikes!" Ricky cried out. "Let's make believe we're pioneers!" He jounced up and down until his brother made him stop. Then, as the road wound around a small pond filled with lily pads, Ricky spied his sisters coming out of the old schoolhouse. The boy put two fingers into his mouth and let out a shrill whistle.

Too late, he remembered the warning the old driver had given him the day before. The oxen stopped short and refused to go forward. Instead, they pulled this way and that, trundling the cart off the road. The beasts stopped knee-deep in the middle of the lily pond as the passengers cried out in fright.

Pete looked about wildly for help. Far down the road he spied Indy chatting with Mr. Marshall. "Indy! Help us!" the boy called out.

The lithe Indian came on a run, waded into the water, grabbed the oxen's reins and led the beasts out of the pond.

"It was my fault," Ricky said, hanging his head

as Mr. Marshall appeared on the scene. "I whistled, but I'll never do that again around the oxen."

The tourists almost got their feet wet, but not quite. They forgave Ricky when he promised them a better ride. Then, as the visitors laughed and chatted, Pete and Ricky took them sightseeing around the grounds.

Meanwhile Emmy drove Indy back to the motel for dry clothes and the girls went exploring. The group had agreed to meet in an hour at the Stagecoach Inn.

The time was almost up when black clouds filled the sky and the wind blew harder and harder. Big drops of water came splashing down, and the girls ran for the Inn.

As they scampered onto the porch a great sheet of rain burst upon the countryside. It grew almost as dark as night.

Moments later the Hollister station wagon came up the hill with its lights on and stopped in front of the building.

As the girls dashed for the car, the boys appeared, running out of the gloom.

"Hurry, get in!" Emmy called. "The hurricane is here!"

As the children piled into the car, Blackie stood on the back seat barking excitedly.

"We just got the oxen into the barn in time," Pete declared.

Indy drove slowly down the narrow dirt road and

up to the top of the next hill. But the rain was coming down so hard that the windshield wipers could not clear his vision.

"It's no use," Indy said and stopped the car. "I can't drive in this storm. We'll have to go inside somewhere and wait."

"We're nearest to the church," Pete said, peering through the streaming windows. "Let's make a run for it."

With Indy carrying Sue, and Pam holding Blackie in her arms, they raced through the downpour. Dripping wet, they stepped inside the church vestibule. Mr. Marshall was there ahead of them.

Pete flicked on his pocket radio. The news was all about Hurricane Cora. "It will probably be the worst in the history of Foxboro," the announcer was saying.

"What'll we do?" Pam asked.

"You'll just have to stay here until it ends," Mr. Marshall said. He and Indy fought their way out into the storm and returned half an hour later with blankets, a flashlight, sandwiches and a big thermos bottle of soup, all covered by a heavy tarpaulin.

"This Cora's going to be a real wildcat," Mr. Marshall declared. "I've got to nail boards over some of the windows in the Village or they'll be smashed to smithereens." Indy offered to help and the men left again at once.

Meanwhile Pete had lit a fire in a big coal stove

Pam made a run for it.

which stood in one corner of the church. The children and Emmy gathered around it and before long their clothes were dry.

By the time they were ready for bed, Indy still had not returned. Now the rain beat against the roof like wind-blown pebbles. Blackie huddled beside Pete and shivered.

"I'm scared, too," Sue declared.

"Don't worry, honey," Pam said, hugging her. "You can sleep next to me."

The blankets were laid out in the church pews, and the children took to their stiff bunks. For a long time they lay awake listening to the rain pelting down. Finally they fell asleep.

Suddenly, in the middle of the night, they were awakened by a strange noise. Pete sat up and listened. The church bell was ringing!

CHAPTER 11

BLACKIE'S DISCOVERY

BONG, *bong!* The sound drifted down through the howling of the storm as the frightened children listened. Who could be ringing the bell, they wondered.

"There's nobody up there," Emmy said, trying to quiet the youngsters.

"Yes, there is!" Ricky insisted. "Why else would the bell ring?"

"Maybe one of the robbers is hiding in the belfry," Holly said.

"But why would he ring the bell," Pam asked, "and give his hiding place away?"

A dozen reasons ran through their minds. Perhaps one of the thieves was decoying Indy and Mr. Marshall away from another building. Or perhaps the thief was injured in some way and calling for help.

"I think we should investigate," Pete said bravely. "I'm game to go into the belfry."

"So am I," Pam declared stoutly.

Both Ricky and Holly said, "Me too!" But Emmy decided that two detectives should be enough.

"Be careful," Emmy said to Pete as she handed him the flashlight.

While the Indian woman cradled Sue in her arms, Pete and Pam went into the vestibule and began to climb an iron ladder which led high into the belfry. They moved up quietly in the darkness, with Pete in the lead. When the boy's hand felt the platform of the belfry, he snapped on his flashlight and the beam crisscrossed the area. No one was in sight.

"Whew!" Pete exclaimed as he climbed onto the landing and helped Pam to his side.

"At least the noise wasn't being made by one of the robbers," she said with a little shudder. "But what's making the bell ring?"

Pete shone the light up over their heads. There was the church bell with a rope hanging down from it. And close by was the end of a long board which had been ripped loose by the hurricane. With each big gust of wind, the board slammed against the bell.

"Crickets!" Pete said. "Am I glad it's only *that!*"

The boy walked back to the iron ladder, called down to the others and told them what had happened. He was just about to descend when Pam reached over and grabbed his arm.

"Wait!" she exclaimed.

"What's the matter?"

Pam stood before a tiny window which looked out over the museum grounds. "The Stagecoach Inn," the girl said. "See that light?"

Through the teeming rain the boy could make out a glimmer of yellow light moving at the entrance to the Stagecoach Inn. "Maybe Indy's over there with Mr. Marshall," Pete said.

"You're right," Pam replied. "I guess I'm just jittery. Let's go back down."

Pete helped his sister onto the ladder, then descended after her.

Pete and Pam returned to their hard beds and the tired, excited children soon fell fast asleep. When they awoke next morning the storm was over, but Indy had not yet returned.

"The poor man must have worked all night," Pam said as she stretched and yawned. "But now maybe we can go back to our motel."

Ricky was the first to run out onto the soggy ground. He came flying back twice as fast, his hair nearly standing on end.

"F-f-flood!" was all he could blurt out at first. "Come look! There's water everywhere!"

With Blackie at their heels, the travelers hastened outside to see a sight they could hardly believe. Only the high spots around the museum grounds showed above the water level. They looked like islands on a lake. The church and the station wagon were surrounded by the flood.

"What happened?" Pam cried. "And where's Indy, and Mr. Marshall? Oh, dear!"

Pete ran inside to get his transistor radio and flicked it on. Then he raced back to the others with breath-taking news. "A dam broke! The whole Foxboro area is flooded!"

As he spoke they could hear the putt-putt of a motor, and around the back of the old church came a motorboat with two policemen in it.

"Are you all right?" the officers shouted.

"Yes, but where are Indy Roades and Mr. Marshall?" Emmy called to them.

"They helped in the rescue all night," one of the policemen replied. He advised Emmy and the Hollisters to remain where they were until the water subsided. "It won't take long for this place to drain off," he said. Then he tossed a cardboard box to Pete. "A few sandwiches and a carton of milk to keep you going," he explained.

"Thank you!" Pam called, and they all waved at the policemen, who continued down the street, now under water. In the distance the children could see other rescue boats plying back and forth, saving people from the flooded houses.

"I'm glad our motel is on high ground," Pete said, "or our belongings would be awful wet."

The young adventurers scouted around their little island and noticed that the water already had started to go down. As a large board floated past, Pete reached out and grabbed it. When he turned it over, he cried out in dismay. On it were the words: DANGER. TRAVEL AT YOUR OWN RISK. It was the same sign he had seen on the covered bridge!

"Look, Pam! I'll bet the bridge has been destroyed."

"Now Mr. Marshall will never get it for the museum," the girl said sadly.

"No, it's probably washed miles down the river by this time," Pete agreed, shaking his head. Just then Blackie began to bark at a bush beside the church. Holly and Sue ran over to him. When they saw what he had discovered, they cried out, their high, piping voices shrill with delight.

"Come, quick, everybody!" Sue called.

Under the bush cowered a little group of wild animals. There were a raccoon, two chipmunks and a fat ground hog with five small whistle-pigs nestled beneath her.

"Aren't they cute!" Holly exclaimed as she squatted down to stroke one of the babies.

"Careful, or the mother may bite you," Emmy warned.

"Oh, I'll bet they're hungry!" Holly said, and ran for the carton of sandwiches.

"These poor animals must have been driven to high ground by the flood," Emmy said.

"Let's all have breakfast together," Pam suggested when her sister had brought the food. Each of the children had a sandwich, and broke off a piece of bread to give to the stranded animals.

Bright wary eyes peered at them from under the branches, but the creatures did not come out.

"Aren't they cute!" Holly exclaimed.

Blackie yapped excitedly and snuffled at the whistle-pig family.

"Stop it," Pete ordered. "You're scaring them!"

As he pulled the dog back, he saw that the leg of one of the baby ground hogs was crooked and swollen. "Look at this," Pete said.

"The poor little thing must have been injured while scrambling to safety," Emmy remarked.

"I know what we can do," Pam said. "I learned it in first aid." Quickly she found two small sticks.

"I need some string," she said, and Ricky fished a piece out of his pocket. Pam took it and bound the ground hog's leg in a splint. Then Holly ran into the church, got the kitty cowbell from her purse and put it around the whistle-pig's neck. "Just so we'll know where he is at all times," she said.

When the tiny creature had been put back with his brothers and sisters, the Hollisters pushed pieces of bread toward the noses of the whistle-pigs. But they would not eat.

"I know just the thing!" Ricky exclaimed, and dashed toward their marooned car. He rushed back with the eye-dropper set he had bought at the white elephant table. "I knew they'd come in handy someday!" the boy declared.

Each of the children took an eye dropper, filled it with milk, and fed the little whistle-pigs a drop at a time.

After a while the raccoon and chipmunks ventured to eat some of the bread. Then they scurried off, but the ground hog family remained. After the milk feeding, the babies seemed stronger. They began to move about and even the little hurt one limped around.

"I'm going to call him Hippity Hop," Sue said, and clapped her hands as she watched the antics of the small woodchucks.

By this time it was mid-morning and the island around the church was growing larger as the water seeped away. Suddenly the children's attention was taken from the animals by the sound of another boat. In it were Mr. Marshall and Indy. They came straight to the front of the church and jumped out, pulling the craft ashore behind them.

"Was the bridge washed out, Mr. Marshall?" Pete asked.

"We don't know yet."

In a babble of words and laughter, the children told about their spooky adventure after Indy had left them the night before.

"And we were scared when we saw the light at the Stagecoach Inn," Pam said, "until we guessed that you two men were there."

Indy and Mr. Marshall looked at each other, perplexed.

"We weren't at the Stagecoach Inn last night," the museum director said.

"You weren't!" Pete exclaimed.

"We didn't go near the place," Indy added. "Tell us about the light."

After Pete and Pam had told their story, Mr. Marshall suggested that they go to the Inn immediately. Looking across the water, the Hollisters could see the old building on an island like theirs.

"There's only room for two of you," Indy said.

"Pete, Ricky—you go with them," Pam urged, and the two boys sprang into the boat. It putt-putted across the water until the bow came to rest on the lawn of the Stagecoach Inn. All four hopped out and ran onto the front porch. Mr. Marshall took a key from a ring hanging on his belt, but Ricky had already pushed open the door.

"Look, it wasn't locked!" the boy cried.

They hurried inside and glanced quickly at the two long columns of wooden Indians.

"Crickets!" Pete cried out. "A couple of them are missing!"

"You're right!" Mr. Marshall said. "Thieves were in here last night."

CHAPTER 12

SUSPICIOUS STRANGERS

THE theft of the wooden Indians shocked the boys. "Look which ones they took!" Ricky blurted. Missing were the two closest to the door—The Settlers' Friend and Patchy.

"I can't understand it," Mr. Marshall said. "Why would anyone want to steal two wooden Indians?"

"And in the middle of the storm!" Indy added.

"Let's search this hall for clues," Pete suggested.

The four examined the room carefully, but found only a few half-dried mud spots on the floor.

"Maybe we'll find tracks outside," Ricky said and raced from the Inn, followed by the other three. But because the ground had been soaked, there was no sign of the thieves' footprints.

"They've all been washed out," Indy said sadly, standing at the water's edge.

"Now what do we do?" Pete asked with a sigh.

"Stay and hunt for the wooden Indians!" came Ricky's quick reply.

"That's okay with me," Indy agreed.

"But first we have to phone Mother and Dad in Shoreham and tell them we're safe," Pete said.

"That's a good idea," Indy remarked.

"I'll stay here and watch for a police boat," Mr. Marshall said, as the other three turned back toward the Stagecoach Inn. Inside they found that the telephone was in order, and a long distance call was put through to Shoreham.

Mrs. Hollister answered, and Pete assured her at once that they were well and safe. "But we've run into a couple of mysteries," he added.

The boy asked if they might stay a few days longer. Mrs. Hollister replied that it was up to Indy, then said she wanted to talk with Ricky.

"Everything's flooded, Mother," the redhead told her. "It's really keen!" Then he asked how Zip, Domingo and the cats were. After reporting that all the animals were well, Mrs. Hollister spoke with Indy, giving permission for her young detectives to remain in New England until their mysteries were solved.

Pete and Ricky looked brighter. They hastened outdoors in time to see a police boat coming close. Two officers were aboard. Mr. Marshall hailed them, and Pete called out to tell of the theft of the wooden Indians. "They just couldn't have walked away by themselves," the boy said.

"Or swum away either," Ricky added.

After promising to be on the alert for the stolen property, the policemen asked Indy and Mr. Marshall if they would continue to help in the rescue operations.

"Glad to," Indy said, "but we must get these two boys back to the old church."

Just as he spoke, another motorboat with a boy at the tiller putt-putted up to the side of the Stagecoach Inn.

"Hi, Pete! Hi, Ricky!" the steersman called out.

"Hello, Wally!" Pete cried. "Is this your boat?"

"Yep! Isn't she a beaut?"

"Yikes!" Ricky exclaimed. "Will you take us back to the church?" He pointed to the island where the girls could be seen running about with Blackie.

"Hop in," Wally said and wiggled his ears.

As the police boat took off with Indy and the museum man, Pete, Ricky and Wally made straight for the church. On the way, the Hollister boys told their chum of the theft. As soon as they reached their own little island the boys relayed the information to the girls and told them of the call to Shoreham.

"Now we have two robberies to solve," Pam said, speaking to the three still in the boat.

"And a quilt to find," Holly added.

"What about the old bridge, Wally?" Pam asked. "Was it washed away?"

"I don't know," he replied. "But we can go over there and take a look."

Pete and Ricky were enthusiastic about the idea. When Pam said that she and the others would stay and tend to the whistle-pigs, the three young sailors skirted the island to the back of the church. There

121

they continued in a beeline over the flooded countryside.

"Yikes, you can't see the river because it's covered up with water!" Ricky exclaimed with a twinkle.

"The bridge should be just ahead!" Wally said, pointing. At first the boys could see only the tops of trees laden with all sorts of debris.

But further on Pete cried, "There it is—still standing!" They sighted the roof of the covered span. It swayed dangerously, looking as though it might be carried downstream at any moment.

Another boat with three men aboard was cruising carefully about the structure. As the boys approached, Wally called out to them, "Is it going to hold, do you think?"

The man in the front of the boat shook his head dubiously. "We're going to blow it up," he said. "We're from the town engineer's office."

Wally cupped one hand to his mouth as he held onto the tiller with the other. "But the museum people want the bridge—"

"Too bad," came the reply. "It'll have to go, for safety's sake."

"Are you going to blow it up right now?" Ricky asked, his eyes popping with excitement.

"No—tomorrow," the spokesman replied. "We have to round up a demolition crew first."

"Crickets," Pete said to his companions, "we'd better find Mr. Marshall and tell him. He might be able to persuade them to wait."

As he finished speaking, Pete stood up to take a better look at the bridge. Just then a long board floated by and banged into their craft. Pete was thrown off balance and pitched toward the swollen, muddy water. But Ricky caught him and both boys landed in the bottom of the boat.

"Whew!" exclaimed Wally. "You almost got it that time, Pete. Don't you know you're not supposed to stand up in boats?"

Pete looked contrite. "I'm sorry, Wally," he said. "I do know better. I shouldn't have taken the chance."

Wally, who had been holding the prow of his craft into the rushing waters, turned it about and chugged downstream a ways. As they passed the old mill, they saw that the ruins were nearly covered by the flood. But a short distance beyond, the waters eddied quietly into a little cove.

"Let's stop here for a while," Pete said. "There's Mrs. Willow's place. I'd like to ask her about the quilt."

"Might as well," Ricky spoke up. "Mr. Marshall's out with the rescue crew, so we probably won't see him until later."

Wally headed into the cove, which normally was a wooded glen running up from the road toward Mrs. Willow's home. He hitched the boat to a tree trunk not far from the house, and the three boys hopped out. As they walked toward the door, Wally held a hand over his eyes and squinted up the hill-

Pete pitched toward the muddy water.

side. Pete and Ricky followed his gaze and saw two men rapidly climbing toward the top. They disappeared into the woods.

"I wonder who they are," Pete said.

"Both of them had big suitcases," Wally remarked.

"They seemed to be in an awful hurry," was Ricky's comment.

Pete rang the jangly doorbell, and in a few moments, Mrs. Willow greeted her three callers. Pete made the introductions, then said, "Our sisters were here looking for a certain quilt. Have you found it yet, Mrs. Willow?"

The woman shook her head slowly. "I haven't had time," she said. "Just as I was about to search for it, two men came to my house for lodging."

"Were those the fellows we saw climbing up the hill?"

"You mean they're gone?" Mrs. Willow asked in surprise. "Well, what do you know about that!" As the boys plied her with questions, Mrs. Willow told them that the men, both with a heavy growth of beard, had come to the house early that morning asking for a place to sleep.

Thoughts of train robbers flashed through Pete's mind, but he said nothing as Mrs. Willow continued.

"They told me their car had been washed away. I felt so sorry for them that I forgot all about looking for the quilt."

"Did they sleep in your house?" Ricky asked.

"No, in the barn," Mrs. Willow said. "Since I didn't know them, I thought that would be wisest."

"Maybe we could see the place," Pete said.

"Of course. Come with me," the stout woman replied. She led the boys around the side of the house to the gray barn.

"Did those men give their names?" Pete asked as Mrs. Willow opened the door.

"No," she said. "I didn't ask them. And I didn't charge them, either, because they slept out here in the hay."

Inside, the barn smelled cool and musty. Mrs. Willow explained that she had not kept animals since her husband passed away several years before. "But we used to have two fine horses and a cow," she said.

Pete glanced about the dim interior as the woman spoke. To one side was a row of stalls, and an old lantern hung on a nail hammered into the center post of the building. A ladder led to the loft and Pete climbed up it. He felt about the hay for any object the men might have dropped, but there was nothing.

"Are you boys trying to find something?" Mrs. Willow asked, puzzled.

"I thought we might pick up a clue as to who those men are," Pete said. "But I guess there isn't— wait!"

As he descended the ladder his eyes focused on

the lantern, and then on the nail which held it. A scrap of gray canvas was snagged on the end of the nail. Pete lifted the fragment off, then went to the doorway to examine the cloth more clearly in the light. It was only as large as the palm of his hand, and had part of the letter S stenciled upon it in black ink. "Could this be part of a U.S. mail sack?" he wondered as the other boys came over.

"Yikes!" Ricky said. "That might be a lead to the train robbers, Pete."

"Maybe the police would like to see it," Wally said. "There goes one of their boats now."

Quickly the Foxboro boy ran down to the water's edge and hailed the police craft. When it landed, Pete told the two officers of his find. One of them, who was carrying a walkie-talkie, got out and examined the cloth.

"I think this *is* part of a postal sack!" he exclaimed. "Our best clue yet!"

CHAPTER 13

STICKS AND PILLOWS

"CRICKETS!" Pete exclaimed. "That means the train robbers were in the barn!"

"We saw them hurrying up the hill!" Ricky added. "And they each had a big suitcase."

"Probably full of the stolen money," said the policeman in the boat.

Mrs. Willow then told about the two men coming to her for lodging.

Quickly the officer with the walkie-talkie called headquarters and reported what he had learned. When he had finished, he said, "We'll search the area right away. The robbers may still be around here."

"Maybe you'll find their abandoned car," Wally said.

"I think not," the man replied as he got back into the motorboat. "That automobile story is probably a hoax."

"If they had a car they'd have used it for a getaway before now," Pete remarked.

As the police craft chugged off, the boys said good-by to Mrs. Willow and hurried to Wally's boat. The front of it rested partly on the ground because the water had receded several feet. After Wally and Ricky stepped aboard, Pete untied the rope and shoved off.

The return to the museum grounds took longer than the outgoing trip. Now there were many little rises of ground showing, and Wally had to steer in and out along a chain of small lakes.

The new route took him past a high platform on the museum grounds which Pete and Ricky had not noticed before. On it were two upright wooden frames. One was tall and had a wide plank across the top with three holes in a row. The other was low and held two boards, each with a pair of holes in it.

"Those are the stocks and pillory," Wally said as the boat glided over a very shallow spot.

"What are they for?" Ricky asked.

"They were used to punish people in colonial days," Wally explained. "The tall one's the pillory. The prisoner had to stand with his head and hands sticking out of those holes so the townspeople could ridicule him."

"It's like a big wooden collar," said Ricky.

"We read about this in school," Pete put in. "Gossips and other troublemakers were put there."

"The low frame is the stocks," Wally went on. "You had to sit behind that with your ankles and wrists in the holes."

As Ricky studied the contraption, he noticed that

the heavy boards looked warped. "How did people get their heads through the holes?" he asked. "There's not much room."

"The top half of the board lifts up and fits down over the neck and wrists," the Foxboro boy said. "The stocks work the same way."

"Yikes, I wouldn't want to be stuck in one of those things," Ricky said as their craft chugged away from the punishment platform.

The water had receded so far from the church that the island had become a hill. There was only a small stream through which Wally could navigate to it.

"I'd better head for my boathouse," he said as Pete and Ricky hopped out.

"Okay, Wally," Pete replied. "Thanks for the ride. We'll see you later."

The brothers watched their friend putt-putt away through the maze of small streams on his way to the river.

When the two boys ran up the slope they found their sisters playing with the whistle-pig family.

"We made them a house," Holly said and pointed to the breakfast carton standing on its side. The mother ground hog and her babies seemed to enjoy the cozy box, even though Blackie romped about and barked playfully.

When Pam asked her brothers about their adventure, Pete quickly told what had happened. He added, "Pam, I think you and I had better try to find Mr. Marshall. Time is important if we want to save that old bridge."

The children found Emmy inside the vestibule of the church setting out a picnic luncheon which had been dropped off shortly before by one of the police boats. Pete and Pam ate sandwiches and milk at once, then quickly set off, following the high ground around the Village in their search for the director.

After the younger children had eaten, Emmy rocked Sue in her arms. The little girl soon fell fast asleep. Ricky and Holly tiptoed away, then raced over the soggy turf in a game of tag. They ran along the ridges until they came to the wooden platform containing the stocks and pillory. Holly stopped short after Ricky had tagged her and pulled her pigtails for good measure.

"What is this?" she asked, looking up.

Ricky threw out his chest and said importantly, "Sticks and pillows. That's where they kept colonial people who talked too much."

"Whizzickers!" Holly said, climbing up on the damp platform.

"I'll tell you all about it," Ricky offered, and repeated what Wally had told him. Then he added with a sly look, "Maybe you'd like to try putting your head through that little round hole."

Holly glanced at the pillory. "It's too high for me, Ricky," she said. "Maybe we could use that thing." She pointed to the stocks.

"Oh, the sticks," Ricky said, as if he knew everything about them. "You just sit down *here*, and put your feet in *there*."

"You do it first and show me how," Holly said, hunching her shoulders as if she were scared.

"Oh, there's nothing to it," Ricky replied. "Watch!" By tugging hard he raised the top half of the heavy foot board. Then he sat down and thrust his feet into the opening. Before he could say another word, Holly put all her weight into one big push and forced the collar down about her brother's ankles.

"Hey, you shouldn't do that," Ricky said.

"You were going to trap me, weren't you?" Holly asked, her eyes dancing.

"Let me out of here!" Ricky demanded, struggling to free his ankles.

"All right," Holly agreed, and tugged at the warped board. But she could not budge it.

"Yikes!" Ricky exclaimed. "I'm glad the water's going down instead of up. Find somebody to get me out of here, Holly!"

As the girl glanced about, a figure came into sight around the corner of a building. "Oh, look, there's Indy," she said, and shouted to him for help.

The Hollisters' friend came at a trot and chuckled when he saw what had happened to Ricky.

"Are you a gossip?" he asked the prisoner.

"Let me out of here!" Ricky demanded.

"No, I'm not," Ricky declared. "Holly just tricked me, that's all."

With a strong pull, Indy raised the board holding the redhead's ankles. Ricky jumped up and was about to pull Holly's pigtails when Indy scooped the little girl up in his arms.

"The joke was on you, Ricky," he said, and tousled the boy's head. Then he set Holly down and the three hastened back toward the old church. There they found Pete and Pam, who had just returned from the Stagecoach Inn where they had found the museum director.

"Mr. Marshall is going to do all he can to stop the men from blowing up the bridge tomorrow," the boy said.

"Maybe the water's low enough so that it's no longer a menace," Indy suggested. Then he told of his rescue experiences that day and how he had saved a kitten from the top of a barn. Finally Indy smiled, showing his white teeth. "I have some other news, too," he reported.

"Somebody else was saved?" asked little Sue.

When Indy nodded, Pam said, "Is it somebody we know?"

The man burst out laughing for he could keep the secret no longer. "Patchy, the wooden Indian. The police fished him out of the river about ten miles below here at a place called Pine Haven."

"That's a long way to swim," declared Sue.

"But what about the other Indian?" asked Ricky. "Where's The Settlers' Friend?"

Indy said nothing had been seen of the second wooden figure. The police had surmised that the thieves, having been caught in the flood, let the statues float away.

"Then we ought to go get Patchy as soon as we can," Pete said. "Maybe we'll find some clues on him to help us catch the thieves!"

"I've already told the police we'd pick him up," said Indy. "We'll go right after supper." By now the water had gone down enough so that the station wagon could be driven to the motel. There the travelers took hot showers and put on fresh clothes. Later they ate supper at the coffee shop. Then, while Sue and Blackie remained at the motel with Emmy, the others drove toward Pine Haven.

Pam, seated in front between Indy and Pete, unfolded a road map on her lap. She followed the twisting route with her finger. Finally she said, "It's just about two miles ahead."

Minutes later they arrived at a small town. It consisted of nothing more than a main street with a few stores and a gasoline station. Indy pulled up in front of the gas pumps and a man approached him in overalls.

"Will you direct me to the police chief?" Indy asked.

"That's me," the attendant said, wiping his hands on a rag.

"We're looking for the wooden Indian that was washed down the river," Pete spoke up.

"You've come to the right place," the man said with a grin. "He's inside."

The children hopped out of the car and followed Indy into the gas station. There was Patchy, still damp and still wearing the fierce expression which had startled Pam in Shoreham.

"That's the one we're looking for," Pete said, "but where's his rifle?"

"Search me," the police chief replied. "He didn't come with any rifle."

"Yikes!" Ricky said. "Maybe it floated away."

Pam looked disappointed. "That will spoil his looks," she said. "Oh, I do wish we could find it!" She explained who they were and added, "We'd like to take the Indian back to the Stagecoach Inn."

"Good," said the police chief-gas station man. "I was hoping someone would call for him." Then he promised to let the museum know if he found the wooden rifle.

Patchy was once again lashed to the top of the station wagon and the travelers started toward Foxboro.

Halfway there it grew dark and Indy switched on the lights. Bright beams showed a huge puddle in the road ahead. As he pulled to the right, the back wheel of the car bogged down into soft mud by the roadside.

"I should have known better," the driver muttered as he and the children got out of the car to look. "I think if we all push and somebody steers, we can get out of here okay," Indy said. He turned to Holly. "You get in there and drive," he said. "Step on the gas, but do it *slowly.*"

Indy and the others put their shoulders against the back of the car and made ready to shove hard. Inside, Holly gripped the steering wheel and stretched her right foot forward until it reached the gas pedal.

"Easy now! Slowly!" Indy called out. "Go ahead, Holly!"

The little girl applied her toe gently to the accelerator, but as she did she slipped forward on the smooth seat. Her foot hit the gas pedal hard! The back wheels spun, sending up a shower of mud!

CHAPTER 14

TWELVE COWS

THERE were loud yells as Pete, Pam, Ricky and Indy were splattered by the cold wet mud.

"Stop, Holly!" shouted Pete as he jumped away from the spinning wheels of the car.

"Take your foot off the gas!" bellowed Indy. The back tires stopped whirling in the mud puddle. Holly jumped out of the car and ran toward them.

"I'm sorry—I couldn't help it," she said, and stopped short at the sight before her. In the dim light of the tail lamps, four mud-spattered figures stood glaring at her.

"I told you to step on the gas easy!" Indy said.

"I know," said Holly in a little voice. "But my foot slipped. I'm sorry," she added, but her face split into a grin and she began to laugh.

"Yikes!" said Ricky hotly. "It isn't funny."

"Oh!" gasped Holly. "If you could only see yourselves!" She giggled till the tears ran down her face.

The bedraggled foursome looked at one another, and Pete began to chuckle. In a few moments all of them were laughing. When they had caught their breath and were once again ready to try to move the car, Pam said, "This time I'll step on the gas!"

The others pushed and finally the car rolled out of the mud. In a few minutes the travelers were on their way back to the motel.

"Yikes!" said Ricky. "This mud is making my face all stiff. I can't even move my eyebrows."

Holly giggled. "Maybe it'll make you beautiful. Some ladies go to the beauty parlor for mud packs!"

When the group arrived at the motel they saw a light on in Emmy's room. Ricky was first out of the car. He ran to the door, knocked loudly, then peered in the window.

Sue and Emmy were sitting on the bed. The little girl glanced up and saw a brown-spotted face looking in at her. She screamed and threw her arms around the Indian girl, shutting her eyes tightly.

"My goodness!" exclaimed Emmy as she hurried to the door. "What ever happened?" she asked when she opened it.

"It was Holly's fault," said Ricky promptly. "But she couldn't help it."

As the other mud-stained travelers stepped in, Sue peeked at them from behind Emmy's skirts. But the little girl began to giggle when they told what had happened. Emmy laughed too. "Well, you'll have to get cleaned up right away," she said, shaking her head. "I can see that tomorrow is going to be a wash day!"

Next morning as they were finishing breakfast, Pete and Indy decided to take the wooden Indian back to the museum.

"I'd rather play on the jungle gym," Ricky said.

"I'll help Emmy wash those muddy clothes," Pam volunteered.

"Me too," spoke up Holly. "There's a coin laundry right in the motel. It'll be fun."

Before Emmy could say anything, the door to the coffee shop opened and Zuzu skipped in. "Hello!" she said cheerfully. "I've come to play with you!" Under one arm she had a shoe box and under the other a large tablet.

Seeing Pam hesitate, Emmy spoke up at once. "I'll do the laundry. You girls run along and take Sue with you."

"Let's draw pictures," said Zuzu. She opened the shoe box and showed them that it was full of crayons.

As Pete and Indy headed for the station wagon, the girls and Ricky went around to the play yard behind the motel. Ricky climbed up on the jungle gym, and the girls started to draw at a little table nearby.

For a while, Pam watched Zuzu coloring her picture. Then she decided to question her about the robbers the child said she had seen at the mill.

"After all," Pam thought, "she *might* have been telling the truth."

Before Pam could speak, Holly looked at Zuzu's paper and asked, "Who's that?"

"It's my fairy godmother," the child replied. "She's riding on a white horse."

"Now Zuzu," said Holly in a grown-up voice, "you know you don't have a fairy godmother."

"Yes, I do," said Zuzu dreamily, "and I live in a castle, too. Sometimes my fairy godmother takes me for a ride on her white horse in the moonlight."

When Pam heard this, she decided it was no use to question the child about the robbers. "She probably made up the whole thing," Pam thought.

"Yikes!" Ricky exclaimed. "What a whopper you told, Zuzu!"

"It's really and truly true," replied the child.

Ricky stood up in the rings. "Nobody has a fairy godmother!" he declared.

"*I* do!" insisted Zuzu.

"Let's have a contest," said Pam quickly, trying to avoid an argument. "We'll see who can draw the best cow."

For five minutes the girls were quiet and busy.

"Time's up!" said Pam. "Now we'll vote." Each girl showed her picture. But Sue's paper had only a red barn on it.

"You're out, Sue," said Holly. "You were supposed to draw a cow."

141

"I drew twelve of 'em," replied her sister.

"Where are they?" demanded Holly.

"In the barn," declared the little girl. "Do I win?"

The other girls laughed and voted to let her win.

"All right. Here's the prize," Pam said. She took a package of peppermints from her pocket and after giving two of them to Sue, passed the package around.

The rest of the morning the children played together happily. At noon Emmy called them for lunch.

"Zuzu," she said, "I telephoned your mother and she said that you could eat with us in the coffee shop, but you must go home right afterward."

When lunch was over, Emmy gave Pam, Holly and Ricky permission to walk to the museum.

On the way they dropped Zuzu off at her house. Mrs. Culver was in the front yard cutting flowers.

"Did you have a nice time?" she asked her daughter.

"Yes," said the child. She thanked the Hollisters for lunch, said good-by, and skipped around the side of the house.

"Did Azuba tell you any stories?" asked Mrs. Culver.

"Yes," Ricky said. "All about her fairy godmother."

The woman looked worried. "I was afraid of that. You see," she explained, "one of our neighbors has a white sports car. Several evenings ago she gave Azuba a ride in it. And out of that Azuba made up the fairy godmother story."

"She has a wonderful imagination," said Pam. "Maybe she will grow up to write stories."

"Perhaps," said her mother. "But first she must learn that there is a time and a place for stories. Now no one knows when to believe her."

After saying good-by to Mrs. Culver, the Hollisters walked across the street to the museum. When they arrived at the Stagecoach Inn, they saw their station wagon parked in front.

Inside, Patchy was standing in his accustomed place. But neither Indy nor Pete was there. As the children were leaving they met Mr. Marshall coming in the front door. He told them that Pete and Indy had eaten lunch with him.

"Your brother's gone up to the old church to see how the whistle-pigs are getting along," the museum man said cheerfully. "And Indy is looking for a rifle similar to the one the wooden Indian had."

"A real one?" Ricky asked.

"Indy thinks we could use a real one as a model for a wooden one. He thought perhaps you boys might like to whittle a gun for the Indian."

"That would be great!" Ricky said. "I—" he

143

was interrupted by the ringing of the telephone beside the door.

"Excuse me," Mr. Marshall said, and answered it. As he listened to the voice on the other end, his face fell. After a few moments he said good-by quietly and hung up. Then he turned to the children and gave a big sigh. "I'm afraid that's the end of the bridge," he said.

"Oh, no!" cried Pam. "Are they going to blow it up?"

Mr. Marshall nodded. "I pleaded with the mayor and the town engineer, but the council has voted to destroy it."

"That's awful," said Holly. "We were hoping you could talk them out of it."

"When are they going to do it?" asked Ricky.

"The engineer is setting up a work crew now," was the reply.

"Oh, but there must be some way to save the bridge!" exclaimed Pam. "Maybe if you offered to pay to have it made safe right away—"

Mr. Marshall shook his head. "I've tried that. It's no use. The trouble is that until the will is settled, no one knows who owns the bridge. Since it doesn't belong to the museum, I have no right to fix it."

"But there's still a chance that the will is good and you can buy the bridge!" Pam exclaimed. "We know where there might be a friendship quilt that belonged to Patience Jones."

"And maybe her signature's on it," Holly put in.

"Come on," said Pam to the other children. "We must go to Mrs. Willow's right away."

"Maybe Indy could drive us," Holly suggested.

"It would take too long to find him," Ricky said. "Is there a short cut?" he asked Mr. Marshall.

The museum director looked surprised, but he told them to go up to the church and down the hill behind it. "That'll bring you to the covered bridge," he said. "There'll probably be a couple of boats in the river and one of them may take you across. If not, you'll have to walk down to the main bridge and cross over to Old Mill Road."

The children quickly left the Stagecoach Inn and ran up the muddy hill. When they reached the church, they saw Pete beside the ground hogs' carton.

"Hurry up!" the older boy called when he saw them. "The whistle-pigs are leaving! I'm going to follow them!"

Panting, the other three caught up to their brother and told him about the bridge.

"Crickets!" Pete exclaimed. "We've got to get to Mrs. Willow's as fast as we can!"

"Look! The whistle-pigs are going the same way," Ricky said. He pointed to the mother ground hog, who was galumphing toward the brow of the hill with her babies strung out behind her.

"The whistle-pigs are leaving!"

The Hollisters ran after the woodchucks. Going down the slope, Pete and Pam sped past the younger children and the animals.

"Wait!" Holly called. "Look!" Pete and Pam paused to glance back. The mother whistle-pig was heading for a hole in the hillside.

"She's going in!" Ricky called. The fat creature ducked her head, started into the burrow, but stopped. Her brown rump remained above ground. Then the woodchuck backed out of the hole. Once again she went part way, and again backed out.

"She can't get in!" called Holly.

"Maybe some other animal is in the burrow," Pam replied.

The little whistle-pigs were huddled together nearby, watching their mother.

"But now they have no home," Holly said sadly to Ricky.

"Let's go back and get their box," he suggested. Then he called to Pete and Pam, "You go on to Mrs. Willow's."

The older children took off down the hill. When they reached the river bank, there was no boat in sight. Both of them eyed the rickety bridge.

"Shall we risk it?" Pete asked.

"It'll take too long to go to the main bridge," Pam replied.

Crossing their fingers, the children stepped onto the unsteady span. They picked their way carefully through the dimness, holding their breath

147

as they walked on shaky boards. Underneath they could hear the rushing of the still-swollen river.

Finally they reached the other end, came out into daylight again, and soon reached the old mill.

Suddenly Pete grasped Pam's sleeve. "Wait!" he said to her. "I think I heard something inside there!"

Both children stood still and listened. "It was a thump," Pete said softly, then added, "I'm going to take a quick look around here. You go on to Mrs. Willow's."

As Pam ran ahead, her brother walked quietly to the ruined stone wall. There he paused under a tree to listen again. The ground was littered with flood debris, and Pete noticed several large pieces of lumber caught in the branches overhead. But there was no sign of life.

A moment later something heavy hit the back of Pete's neck, and the boy fell to the ground unconscious.

CHAPTER 15

A MYSTERIOUS THEFT

WHEN Pete's eyes finally fluttered open, he did not know what had happened. Then the ache at the back of his neck reminded him of the sudden blow that had knocked him out.

Carefully he sat up and saw that he was in the high grass at the edge of Old Mill Road.

"Crickets!" he thought. "How did I get here?" The last he remembered he had been standing under a tree near the mill. Had someone carried him to the roadside?

Pete stood up unsteadily and looked around. He was a short distance from the old ruin. There was no one in sight.

The boy guessed that a piece of the lumber had fallen from the tree and hit him on the back of the neck. "I must have been stunned, walked up here and collapsed," he thought.

Remembering that Pam would be wondering what had happened to him, Pete started down the road toward Mrs. Willow's house. By the time he had climbed her hill and rung the doorbell, the ache in his neck was going away.

It was Pam who answered the door. As soon as she saw her brother's face she knew something was wrong.

At the same time Mrs. Willow waddled into the hallway. "My goodness, boy!" she exclaimed. "You're white as a sheet!"

When Pete told what had happened, Mrs. Willow put her plump hand on his brow. "Have you a fever?"

"No, I'm fine, thank you," Pete said hastily. "Did you find the friendship quilt?"

"Not yet," replied Pam. "We've been looking through the downstairs closets."

"Oh, it's here somewhere," Mrs. Willow said. "If I could just remember where."

"You said you have trunks of quilts in the attic," Pam reminded her. The stout woman hesitated.

"Yes," she said. "But I was hoping we wouldn't have to climb all those stairs."

"But we must find that quilt, Mrs. Willow. Please!" Pete said.

"There's no time to lose," Pam added.

"All right," the woman said with a sigh. "Come along." She led the way to the staircase. Holding on to the banister with one hand, she began to climb slowly. Following the huge woman, Pete and Pam exchanged worried looks. By this time the work crew was probably on its way to blow up the bridge.

Finally Mrs. Willow reached the top of the nar-

150

row attic stairs, opened the low door, and entered with the children at her heels. Their steps echoed on the bare wooden floors as they crossed a large, dim room crowded with furniture and trunks. At the far end they stopped beside a bull's-eye window which let in a shaft of sunlight. Nearby were two old round-topped trunks.

"I keep my quilts in these," Mrs. Willow said, puffing. She bent over and tugged at the lid of one of the trunks. It did not open.

"That's funny," she remarked. "I didn't think I locked it. But maybe I did." She sighed. "I'll have to go downstairs and look for the key."

Pete groaned inwardly. "Let us try to open it, Mrs. Willow," he said. Quickly he and Pam tugged hard at the lid of the trunk. With a creak and a scrape it came up. Then Pete opened the second trunk. Each of them was piled high with quilts.

Mrs. Willow's eyes brightened at the sight of the coverlets. "Children," she said, "every one of those quilts has a history. As soon as I catch my breath, I'll tell you about each one."

"Oh," thought Pam, "we'll never get through them all in time!" Then she said, "Mrs. Willow, why don't you sit down and rest? You can tell us about the quilts some other day."

"That's very thoughtful of you," said the stout lady. She dusted off a nearby rocking chair and settled herself in it. As her chair creaked back and forth, Pete and Pam examined each coverlet. By the time they had reached the bottom of the second trunk they were hot, dusty and discouraged. Nowhere had they found Patience Jones's signature.

Deeply disappointed, the children put the bedcovers back in the trunk.

"Please, Mrs. Willow," Pam said, "try to think whether you have quilts anywhere else."

The stout lady stopped rocking and puckered her brow.

"No," she said finally. "I can't remember any others."

While the woman was speaking, Pete had been gazing out the window at Old Mill Road far below. Now he suddenly said, "Pam, look—quick!"

His sister hurried to his side. Going down the road toward the covered bridge was a pickup truck. On the side of it were the words: TOWN OF FOXBORO.

"That's the work crew!" Pete cried out. "They're going to blow up the bridge right now!"

"If only we could stop them," Pam exclaimed.

"Maybe if I tell them how hard we are searching for the quilt," Pete said, "they'll hold off for a little while."

"I don't think it's much use," said Mrs. Willow.

"Neither do I," Pete called back as he dashed toward the door, "but I'm still going to try." A moment later they heard him pounding down the stairs. Quickly Pam thanked Mrs. Willow for her help and ran after her brother. But in her haste she slipped on the attic stairs and fell several steps to the bottom.

For a few minutes Pam's ankle hurt so badly that she clenched her fists to keep from crying. By the time she got to her feet and was standing on one leg by the staircase, Mrs. Willow had lumbered down to her.

"Are you hurt, child?" she asked in a frightened voice.

"I twisted my ankle," Pam replied. Carefully she put weight on her foot and found she could hobble.

"You come and lie down," Mrs. Willow said, steering Pam into a room across from the stairs.

"No, please," the girl said. "I want to go with Pete. I'll be all right."

But the woman paid no attention. She walked heavily to a big brass bed with a plain blue coverlet on it. "Now, you just rest here until you feel better," she said kindly. With that she grasped the bedcover and threw it back.

Pam was about to protest, but the words died on her lips. The underside of the coverlet was patchwork!

"It's a friendship quilt!" Pam cried. She limped to the bed and examined the patches. There, in

"We've found it!" Pam exclaimed.

one square, written in faded ink, was the signature of Patience Jones!

"We've found it!" Pam exclaimed. "Oh, Mrs. Willow, I must take it to Pete right away!"

"All right," the woman agreed. Before she could say more, Pam scooped up the quilt and, calling thanks and good-by, hobbled from the room.

By the time Pam was downstairs and outside, she was able to run down the hill. Pete was nowhere in sight.

"He must have caught up with the men by now," she thought. When she turned down the lane to the bridge, she saw her brother there, pleading with three workmen.

"Pete! Here it is!" she cried, running to them. Moments later she poured out her story breathlessly.

The foreman was a husky man with carrot-colored hair and friendly blue eyes. "I'd like to help you young people," he said. "But my orders are to dynamite this bridge, and that's what we're going to do."

"Oh, we've tried so hard to save it!" Pam said. In spite of herself, her eyes filled with tears. "Won't you please telephone your office and tell them we found the signature?"

The foreman's face softened. "Well, all right," he said. "I'll see what they say." He went to the truck, took a walkie-talkie from the front seat, and spoke into it quietly.

When he turned back to the children he was smiling. "Okay, little princess," he said to Pam. "I'm supposed to bring you and the quilt to the engineer's office in Town Hall. I guess the old bridge has a little time yet."

"You don't need me," Pete said to his sister. "There's something I want to do at Mrs. Willow's."

The foreman helped Pam into the front seat of the truck, and the other men swung aboard the back. As it rumbled off toward town, Pete walked down the lane behind it. When he reached Mrs. Willow's house, he saw the stout lady in her backyard.

"What happened?" she called to Pete.

After he had told her, he said that he would like to look inside the barn again. "Maybe I could find a clue to those fellows who stayed there," he said.

The woman watched while Pete searched the hay loft and the animal stalls, but he found nothing. Then in one corner he discovered a large cardboard carton. It was open and there were some dresses lying partly out of it.

"Why, those are the clothes I intended to send to charity!" exclaimed Mrs. Willow. "But someone has pulled them out."

"Perhaps those two men took them out to sleep on," Pete guessed. Mrs. Willow sorted through the clothing.

"I can't recall if anything's missing," she said. Then a surprised look crossed her face. "That reminds me," she added, "there *is* something missing. A few tools have vanished!"

She led Pete into a shed beside the barn. On the workbench was a neat row of tools.

"What's been taken?" Pete asked.

"The brace-and-bit, chisel and saw."

Pete looked around and saw a row of paint cans on a shelf. One in the middle was missing. Mrs. Willow followed his glance. "Yes," she said. "The shellac is gone and some brushes, too."

"You'd better report the theft to the police," Pete said, and the woman promised she would. Then he added, "I wonder why those fellows needed tools and shellac."

On the way home, the boy continued to puzzle over the question. As he passed the mill there was a sudden noise in the high grass near the water's edge. Pete stopped short, his heart pounding. A moment later he heard a splash and saw a sleek brown body swimming away from the bank.

"A beaver!" he exclaimed with a grin. "Crickets, am I jumpy!"

Pete hastened on and gingerly crossed the rickety bridge. With a sigh of relief he came out the other side and hurried up the hill.

Near the ground hogs' hole he saw the carton Ricky and Holly had left. There was food in it, but the little animals were gone.

As Pete wondered where they were, he heard the tinkling of a tiny bell. A moment later a baby whistle-pig poked its head out of the burrow. In its mouth was a ten-dollar bill.

CHAPTER 16

HALF A TREASURE

PETE stared at the little animal. Then he reached down, grasped the baby whistle-pig and took the ten-dollar bill from its mouth. He released the creature, and it scampered into the carton beside the hole.

Pete was so excited he hardly noticed. Quickly he knelt beside the burrow, thrust in his arm, and brought out a handful of paper money.

Speechless, the boy looked at it. Mingled with the bills was damp sawdust.

"Crickets!" he finally burst out. "No wonder the big whistle-pig couldn't go in there. The hole is full of money!"

Quickly Pete tucked the bills back into the burrow, then covered the entrance with a large stone. He raced up the slope to the old church, but found no one there. Down the hill he sped to the Stagecoach Inn, where he found Holly and Ricky waiting on the long front porch with Indy. His sister jumped up.

"We know all about it!" she exclaimed. "You don't have to tell us anything!"

"You found the quilt," said Ricky. "We know because the mayor telephoned Mr. Marshall to come to the Town Hall and . . ."

"Listen!" Pete broke in. "I found the train robbery money!"

Before the others could say a word, he began to pour out the story of his discovery. When he was finished, Indy dashed inside to telephone.

Fifteen minutes later a squad of policemen carrying spades swarmed past the church and down the hillside behind Pete. The boy led them to the whistle-pigs' home and removed the stone. As Indy, Ricky and Holly looked on, the police chief reached into the burrow and began pulling out money.

The officers dug around the hole, and Ricky found a big stick with which he helped them. One of the policemen stood nearby with a large canvas sack. He and Indy kept a tally of the money that was dumped into it. More and more bills appeared as the men spaded up the earth.

Suddenly one of them called, "There's another hole over here, Chief!" Holly and Pete ran over to look.

"This must be the other end of the whistle-pigs' burrow," the boy said. Some of the officers hastened to it and began digging.

Suddenly there was a shrill whistling. Out of the hole popped the mother ground hog and her babies.

Pete removed the stone.

"Oh, she's scared!" cried Holly. The girl fetched the carton and put it down near the frightened animals. They scampered into it and huddled in the corner with Hippity Hop.

The officers continued to dig. Word of the discovery had spread around Foxboro, and gradually a crowd had gathered. Pete spotted Wally and hailed him.

As the storekeeper's son hurried over to his friend, Ricky ran to join them. Holly followed, carrying Hippity Hop.

When Wally looked into the canvas bag, his ears wiggled up and down. "Great jumpin' bullfrogs!" he exploded. "Why did the robbers hide all this money in the ground?"

"Maybe they were afraid they couldn't escape with it," Pete replied. "After all, there's a tight police cordon around this whole area."

The chief, a husky man with bristly gray hair, was standing near the boys. "That's right," he said. "There are even patrol boats in the river."

"But if the robbers picked up a boat somewhere," Pete remarked, "they could have escaped over the flooded fields."

"You're right," said the police chief, "but we've combed this area several times. Where could the men be hiding?"

"How about the old mill?" Pete suggested.

The chief shook his head. "My men have gone

over it inch by inch. It's one of the first places we searched."

As he spoke, his eyes roved over the woodchucks' torn-up burrow.

Most of the policemen had stopped digging. One of them came over and said, "I think we've found all the bills that were hidden here, Chief."

"But there's still some money missing," spoke up the officer in charge of the canvas bag.

"This is only about half of it," Indy added.

"And we wouldn't have that," the police chief said, "if it weren't for Pete Hollister. You're a mighty alert young man," he told the boy.

The younger children beamed with pride at the compliment to their brother. The police chief glanced at them and smiled. "And you're the two who discovered the map," he said. "I think you are good detectives too."

Ricky flushed with pleasure and Holly looked down at the little woodchuck in her arms.

"We're glad you found the money," she said, "but now the whistle-pigs haven't any home."

"They can dig another hole somewhere," Indy told her. "You'd better say good-by to them now."

"Oh, can't we keep them for a little while yet?" Holly pleaded.

Indy shook his head. "I don't think the motel owner would want a carton full of whistle-pigs in his place," he said.

Holly's face fell and she rubbed her cheek against the woodchuck's soft fur.

"I'll bet Mr. Marshall would let us keep them in the barn," Ricky declared. "After all, Pete and I drove the oxen for him."

"We could leave the woodchucks there on our way back to the station wagon," Pete suggested, "and then pick up Pam at the Town Hall."

Indy agreed but said they must ask Mr. Marshall's permission to keep the animals as soon as they saw him.

Half an hour later the Hollisters, Wally, and Indy met Pam and the museum director coming out of the Town Hall. Before Pete could say a word about the whistle-pigs, Mr. Marshall grasped his hand and shook it warmly. "I owe you thanks," he declared. "You've saved the bridge."

"The signature on Patience Jones's will is the same as the one on the quilt!" Pam declared happily. "That means the will is good, and Mr. Marshall can buy the bridge."

"I have already paid to have it strengthened," the museum man said. "Work will begin on this tomorrow. As soon as the sale is complete, the bridge can be moved to Pioneer Village."

"That's keen!" exclaimed Holly, and before anyone else could speak, Ricky burst out with the news of the money Pete had found.

Pam beamed. "This has been a day of surprises," she remarked.

Mr. Marshall smiled and rested a hand on Ricky's head. "You have all been very helpful," he said. "I'd like to do something for you."

Holly spoke up. "May we keep the whistle-pig family in your barn until we go home?"

The museum director grinned. "Young lady, you may keep an elephant in there if you want!"

When the happy day was over and the Hollisters were in their beds, Pam was too excited to sleep. Over and over she thought about the missing money and the mystery of the stolen Indian. It was midnight when Pam dozed off, wondering where the train robbers were hiding.

Suddenly she awoke with a start. Someone was rapping softly on the outside door!

CHAPTER 17

SECRET IN THE MILL

PAM sat up in bed and listened. Again came the tapping at the door. "Who could it be?" she wondered.

Pam slid her feet into her slippers, hastened to the window and looked out. The night was moonless and inky dark. She could see nothing.

Holly, too, had awakened. "Are you going to open the door?" she whispered.

The rapping came again.

"Get the boys," Pam said, "and tell them to be quiet. We don't want to wake Sue." When Holly returned with her brothers the knocking was louder.

"Who's there?" Pete called as he tied his bathrobe.

"It's Zuzu!" came a faint voice. Quickly Pete opened the door and the little girl stepped in. She was dressed in a pink bathrobe over a long nightie which nearly hid her fuzzy white bedroom slippers. The Hollisters stared at her, astonished.

"Zuzu!" Pam exclaimed. "What in the world are you doing here at this hour?"

"You were very naughty to come," Holly said

sternly. "What if your mother wakes up and finds you're gone? Besides," she added, "weren't you scared?"

"It was a little scary," Zuzu admitted, "but I have something very important to tell you."

"What is it?" Pete asked.

"I woke up a while ago," Zuzu replied, "because the dog next door was barking. I went to the window to look out, and guess what I saw?"

"What?" the Hollisters asked.

Zuzu's big eyes sparkled and she took a deep breath. "I saw two men walking down the street."

"Is that all?" Holly broke in.

"No. They were carrying another man," the child went on. "One held his head, and the other, his feet. They took him into the museum grounds."

"Gee whizzickers yikes!" Ricky said. "Another whopper!"

Pam cocked her head and looked hard at the little girl. "Zuzu!" she said warningly. "Are you sure you're telling the truth?"

"'Course I am," the child replied. "Don't you believe me?"

The Hollisters looked at Zuzu uncomfortably. Holly said, "Maybe you just imagined it."

"No, I didn't," the child replied. "I really and truly saw the men. And I came all the way up here to tell you about it, so I could be a detective like you are. Please believe me."

Pete shook his head. "Come on, Zuzu," he said. "Pam and I will take you home."

Zuzu's chin quivered and tears spilled from her eyes. "I want to be a detective," she sobbed as Pam led her out the door.

By the time Pete and the two girls reached the bottom of the hill, Zuzu had stopped crying. Pam found a tissue in the pocket of her bathrobe and wiped the little girl's eyes.

"We'd like to believe you, honey," she said. "But you've told us too many fairy stories."

Without replying the child pulled away and ran into the house.

The next morning the travelers slept late. While they were having waffles in the coffee shop, the children told Indy, Emmy and Sue about their night visitor.

"Zuzu's story is hard to believe," Indy agreed.

Just as the children had started second helpings, the door to the coffee shop opened and Mr. Marshall hurried in.

"I thought I'd find you here," he said. "I couldn't wait to tell you the news! The Settlers' Friend is back!" The man looked at the surprised faces of his listeners and chuckled. "There he was, on the porch of the Stagecoach Inn when I arrived this morning. Don't ask me how he got there. All I know is, he didn't walk!"

Quickly Pam put down her fork and stood up. "Zuzu must have been telling the truth!" she exclaimed. "The men she saw were carrying the Indian!" Swiftly Indy explained to Mr. Marshall what Pam meant.

"Please, Emmy," the girl went on, "may I be excused right away? I want to apologize to Zuzu."

"We'd all better go," Ricky said glumly and Emmy gave permission.

The Hollisters found the child in her backyard. Pam told her what had happened and they all said they were sorry they had not believed her.

"I know it's my own fault," Zuzu said. "I'm not going to tell pretend stories any more."

"Was there anything you saw last night," Pete asked, "that you didn't tell us about?"

Zuzu thought for a minute. "The men were carrying a lantern," she said.

"Do you remember anything more about them?" Pam prompted.

"No," said Zuzu. She skipped beside Pam as the Hollisters left her yard, and waved good-by at the front gate.

At the general store, the young detectives found Wally flicking the shelves with a long-handled feather duster. His father was waiting on a man at the other end of the counter.

After Pete had told Wally the news about The Settlers' Friend, the customer turned and saw the children. He was the red-headed foreman of the work crew.

"Well, how's my little princess?" he said to

Pam. Without waiting for an answer, he went on, "We're strengthening the bridge this morning, but I come here to get a new lantern. Somebody the one we had at the warning sign."

"...hen?" Pete asked.

"...st night."

"Crickets!" Pete exclaimed. "The two men who ...urned the Indian to the museum were carrying a lantern. I'll bet they stole it from the bridge!"

"And that's near the mill," Pam said thoughtfully. "I'm still suspicious of that old ruin. Zuzu said she saw the robbers there. Maybe she was telling the truth that time."

"Do you think they're hiding in the mill?" Ricky asked.

"I don't know," Pete replied, "but something queer is going on there. I'm going to search the place."

Wally asked his father's permission to go with the Hollisters. In a few minutes the five children were hastening up the hill to the motel.

Indy did not share their hope of finding anything, but agreed to drive them to the mill. Pete quickly got his flashlight and all the travelers set off together. On the way Indy dropped Emmy, Sue, and Blackie at the museum. "We'll pick you up here when we come back," he promised.

As the station wagon drew near the mill, Pete suggested that they park and approach quietly on foot. Indy pulled off the road and they all got out. With Pete in the lead, the search party made its way through the trees toward the side of the mill. At the edge of the marshy grass, Pete signaled a halt.

Before them lay the tree-shaded ruin, its stone walls dappled by the noon sunlight. Nothing moved. The children listened carefully. There was no sound but the rushing of the river and twittering of birds.

Quietly Pete instructed Holly, Ricky and Wally to station themselves outside the mill. "Whistle if anybody comes," he said. "Pam and I will go inside."

"I'll stand at the door," Indy said with a smile. "Good luck."

Pete and Pam found the wooden door ajar. It yielded to the boy's push and swung open with a creak. The brother and sister stepped into a cool, dim room with a single window. It was filled with debris from the flood. In one corner was an open staircase. One flight led to the second floor, another to the cellar.

The children picked their way across the room and peered down. Rickety steps led into the blackness below.

"I'm going down," Pete said. As he took the flashlight from his belt, Pam seized his arm.

"Look!" she exclaimed and pointed to a pile of

"I'm going down," Pete said.

debris. Sticking out of it was Patchy's missing rifle!

Quickly the children sorted through the junk, which was mixed with sawdust and wood shavings. They turned up an empty shellac can, brushes, brace-and-bit, saw and chisel.

"This is the stuff the train robbers took from Mrs. Willow's place!" Pete whispered hoarsely.

"So they must be the ones who stole the Indians," said Pam. Then she gave a little gasp. "Pete! I think I know where the rest of the stolen money is!"

Pam seized her brother's hand, and together they ran from the mill with Pete clutching the wooden rifle.

Outside, they told the others of their find.

"Well, where *is* the money?" Indy asked.

"The Settlers' Friend has it," said Pam.

"You mean," Indy continued, "that the robbers hollowed out the Indian and hid the money inside?"

Pam nodded.

"I sure hope you're right!" said Wally, wiggling his ears faster than ever.

Now Indy beamed at his young friends. "Let's hurry back to the museum and find out," he said excitedly. "I'll tell the police, too. They'll want to search the mill again."

"Good," said Pete. "Wally, Pam and I will keep

173

watch until they arrive. After all, the robbers may come back here."

"Remember you're no match for them," Indy warned. "If they do show up, run for it!"

After Indy, Ricky and Holly had hurried away, taking the rifle, Pete said, "I'd like to have a look in that cellar. Let's explore while we're waiting."

As the three children walked quietly toward the mill, they heard faint shouts from the bridge crew working on the far side of the river. Pete pushed open the creaking door again, and they entered the gloomy mill.

"Leave the door the way we found it," he said softly to Pam. As she shut it almost all the way, it creaked again.

"What's upstairs?" Wally asked.

"Let's look there first," suggested Pam.

The children went up the narrow wooden stairway and entered a small room almost filled by a huge grinding stone. Suddenly there was a rustling noise downstairs.

"What was that?" Pam whispered.

"Maybe a rat," Wally said softly. Pam shuddered.

With Pete in the lead, they tiptoed out the door and looked down the stairs. Pam cried out in alarm. Climbing out of the window was a bulky woman wearing a big floppy hat!

"Stop!" Pete shouted. The figure in the window

gave a startled jerk, held onto the hat and disappeared.

"After her!" Pete shouted. The children pounded down the steps and out of the mill in time to see the fugitive running toward the bridge.

"There's another one!" Wally cried. In the distance a second long-skirted figure was getting into the workmen's truck. The bulky woman just ahead leaped over a pile of stones, clutching frantically at her clothes.

Money was dropping from her dress!

"They're the bank robbers!" Pete shouted.

The children had nearly caught up to the running thief when he climbed into the pickup beside his confederate.

The motor roared. "Stop!" Pete shouted, and jumped in front of the truck. But instead, it shot forward.

CHAPTER 18

DRESS-UP VILLAINS

PETE leaped aside and the truck roared past him. The children raced down the lane after it. At Old Mill Road they stopped and watched helplessly as it sped toward Foxboro. Just then a blue car appeared, heading in the same direction.

Pete, Pam and Wally dashed out, waving wildly at the approaching motorist. As the young driver slowed to a stop, he called, "What's the matter?"

"We have to catch that truck!" Pete said. "The train robbers are in it!"

For a moment the man did not know whether to believe them. But seeing their excited faces, he said, "Okay. Jump in." As he drove swiftly along Old Mill Road, the children told him what had happened.

"We're gaining on 'em!" cried Pete as they followed the pickup onto the modern bridge. When they reached Foxboro, the young man pulled over to the curb. "Hop out and call the police," he said to Wally. "We'll keep going."

The boy jumped out and the car roared ahead.

When it reached the outskirts of town, the blue car was right behind the pickup. Suddenly the truck swerved to the side of the road and stopped near the ski lift. The blue car did the same. The robbers jumped from the truck cab, picked up their skirts and ran toward the chair lift. The children raced after them.

With a flying tackle, Pete brought down the first man. The second fugitive fell over them. As he struggled to get up, Pam seized the brim of his hat and jerked it down over his eyes. Tripping on his dress, he fell again. By the time the thieves were on their feet the young driver had caught up, and a crowd of sightseers had run over from the chair lift to see what was going on. Two police cars pulled up and Wally leaped out followed by half a dozen policemen.

Quickly the officers collared the robbers and the police chief yanked the floppy hats off them. Both prisoners were tall, powerfully built men. One had limp, sandy hair and a long nose. The other was stouter with a black crewcut.

"The money is hidden in their clothes," Pam said. "They dropped some of it near the mill when they ran away." As bundles of bills were removed from the captives' dresses, Pam added, "I'm pretty sure they hid the rest of it in a wooden Indian."

"How about that?" the chief asked the two men sternly. They scowled and refused to say anything.

Pete turned to the police chief. "If you'll take us to the Stagecoach Inn, I think we can prove it."

"Then let's go," said the chief. He and the children thanked the young driver for his help and after a fast ride, both police cars pulled up in front of the Stagecoach Inn. The children dashed inside to the Indian Hall with the officers and prisoners close behind them.

There was The Settlers' Friend on the floor with Ricky and Indy pulling handfuls of money out of a hole in its base. Holly, Emmy and Mr. Marshall were watching with Sue in front of them, holding Hippity Hop. Blackie barked wildly at the police.

There followed an excited babble of questions and answers. When the noise died down the two robbers looked pale.

The one with the long nose blinked nervously. "I'll talk," he said. Rapidly he confessed that there were six men in the gang. Two had come to Foxboro first, made a map of the holdup area, and hid it in the motel room. Then they went on to Canada to set up a hiding place.

"After that, Harry, here, and I came with two other fellows," he went on. "We stayed in the same motel as the advance men and studied the map they left for us."

"Thanks to these children, we know all that," said the chief.

"We found the map," Holly spoke up.

They pulled out handfuls of money.

The dark-haired man glared at his companion. "I thought you took it off the mattress, Al."

"I thought *you* did," retorted the long-nosed man.

"We tracked down every person who had stayed in that motel room," the police chief put in, "until we located your accomplices. All of them were caught this morning in Canada."

Harry groaned. "This is all your fault, Al," he said to the other robber. Then he explained that his companion had hurt his foot during the holdup and could not run to the getaway car. "I had to help Al to the mill," he grumbled.

"The fellows who made the map set up a hideout in the cellar there just in case we failed to get away," Al explained. "We had canned goods, suitcases to put the money in, a flashlight, and even a radio."

"But the police searched the mill," Wally said, puzzled.

"We figured they would," Harry replied, "so we took all of our stuff and hid in the tall grass under the old bridge. When the search was over, we moved back."

"In a couple of days my foot was better," Al said, "but we decided to lie low in the mill until the police cordon was lifted. Then we heard on the radio that this area was going to be searched again. We had to get away, but we knew we couldn't pass through the cordon with the loot."

"So you decided to hide the money in the wooden Indians," Pete put in.

The dark-haired robber nodded.

"How did you ever carry away those heavy statues?" Mr. Marshall spoke up.

"We had a terrible time with them," Al admitted. He explained that they had dragged the figures, one at a time, up to the church, rolled them down the hill, then carried them across the bridge to the mill.

"After all that, the dam burst," Harry said unhappily. "We took the suitcases and the big canvas money sack and ran for our lives."

"We found a piece of that bag hanging on a nail in Mrs. Willow's barn," Pete spoke up.

"It tore when we were climbing up to the hay loft," Al said. "Before we left there, we stuffed some of the money into one of the suitcases and the rest of it with the canvas bag into the other."

"Then you stole Mrs. Willow's dresses and tools," Pete put in.

Al nodded. "Our plan was to go back to the mill when the water went down, cut holes in the Indians and hide the money. I got the idea for disguises when we saw the dresses."

"But we found a drifting motorboat," Harry went on, "and decided to make our escape in that right away."

Ricky grinned. "That's just what Pete said you might do."

Harry looked sour. "But we didn't," he said. "The water went down too fast. We were stranded and had to go back to the mill."

"Then we found one of our Indians had floated away," Al said.

"And you couldn't fit all the money into the other," Pam guessed, "so you buried some of it in the whistle-pigs' burrow."

"That's right," replied the man, then added sharply, "how did you know?"

"The children found that, too," said the police chief.

Before either robber could speak, Pam asked, "Why didn't you carry the Indian back to the museum by the short cut?"

"We tried," Harry said, "but we couldn't get up the hill behind the church. It was too muddy and slippery."

"The trip took hours!" Al added. "I thought my arms would break. To make it worse, we'd lost our flashlight in the flood."

"So you stole the bridge lantern," Pete put in.

The robber looked at him in amazement. "You know that, too?"

The police chief smiled. "These youngsters also tipped us off to your mill hideout. The search squad is out there now."

"Nosy kids!" Harry exclaimed bitterly. "We heard them poking around the place this morning while we were in the cellar putting on our disguises.

After they left we started up the steps, but they came back again. As soon as they went upstairs we made a break for it."

"Going through the window slowed us down," Al said. "We didn't want them to hear the door creak."

"Everything would have been all right if it hadn't been for them," Harry growled and turned to Pete. "We saw the lumber fall on you at the mill."

"I couldn't let a kid lie there unconscious," Al said, "so I carried you to the road. We thought this accident might scare you away."

"But you just didn't give up," Harry added with a sigh.

After the prisoners had been led away, Pete picked up the round wooden plug Indy had taken from the base of The Settlers' Friend. Carefully he fitted it into place. Then with Indy's help he set the Indian upright.

"Now we'll send his measurements to Mr. Fritz," Pete said, "and tell him The Settlers' Friend led us into an exciting adventure."

"Patchy did, too," said Holly. She patted the fierce Indian who once more held his rifle.

"And now we can go back to Shoreham," Emmy put in, smiling, "and the whistle-pigs to their home."

Sue held up the woodchuck. "Its leg is all better," she announced.

"I'll take off the splint," Pam said. After she had done so, Holly removed the bell from its neck.

"We'll give this to White Nose," she said.

Then Ricky stuck out his hand to Mr. Marshall. "We had a great time solving your mystery," he said.

The man smiled. "You did such a good job," he replied, "that I will always think of it as *your* mystery."

"Oh, no," piped up Sue. "It should be the whistle-pigs' mystery because they found the money!"

As the others laughed, she held up Hippity Hop and kissed him on the nose.